not so yours truly

WARTS & CLAWS INC SERIES (BOOK 4)

CLIO EVANS

"I think we all deserve someone who wants to be with us." —
Phyllis, The Office

warning!

HR Department:

Dear Reader,
There have been **R**eports of the following in
this office: Voyeurism, blood play, strap
ons, bondage ropes, suspension, mating
bites, taking sexy photos, omega heats,
BDSM, Dom/sub dynamics, spanking, blood
sucking, threesomes, spitting, and more.

If any of this makes you uncomfortable,
please report it to your HR rep
immediately.

Not So Yours Truly—
Warts & Claws Horn-y Resources

CHAPTER ONE

monster monday

EMBER

"NO," I said, giving my sibling a dirty look as we stepped into the elevator.

Cinder let out a frustrated sigh. The parental kind. The one I hated with a passion, even though I still loved them.

Their mates stepped in with us, a muscled manticore and a goth pixie demon whose style I loved.

"Come on, Em," Cinder pleaded, hitting the button.

"I'm not moving in with the three of you," I said, my voice firm.

It had been three weeks since the most recent series of events. It was colder than hell outside, and I was wearing a camel-colored peacoat with a black jumpsuit and polka-dot blouse underneath.

"I'm just concerned," Cinder snapped. "You are an omega. And I can't risk you getting hurt. The only reason I let you—"

I shot them a look that could kill, and Lora let out a small sigh, wrapping her arm around my sibling.

"Cinder, she's going to do what she wants," Lora said. "She's an adult. She will move in with us if she wants. You have to stop treating her like a child. Besides, she has that big interview tomorrow and is already making a name for herself around here!"

Lora winked at me, and I did my best to keep a stoic expression.

Cinder looked down at Lora, their burning violet eyes immediately softening. They hissed between their teeth, about to say something that would probably make the two of us fight, but then the doors slid open.

I was out in the hallway before they could stop me, fighting a smirk despite my annoyance.

I liked Mich and Lora a lot. They had been good for Cinder, and I enjoyed seeing them in love. I loved that Cinder was finally happy, despite their fixation on making sure I was safe.

But I didn't want to be in their nest right now. I wasn't an idiot. The three would be fucking five times a night, and I would hear *everything*.

And even if I didn't, *I would know*.

I shuddered at the thought. I loved sex as much as anyone else, but I didn't want to be anywhere near Cinder's deeds.

Especially on a week like this.

I hadn't been in the office for long, but I was already making waves. Inferna had been giving me small side projects here and there, ones I had been able to add to my list of experiences that I could talk about at the interview.

They had decided to open a position for an overall team

leader, one who would oversee all the teams and report back to Art. I wanted it more than anything else.

I'd been a prisoner for so long. Cinder had done everything in their power to ensure I was safe over the years, going as far as to let my boss's family fake kidnap me to get me out of Alfred's crossfire. They had done everything in their power to protect me, but now? Now I was free from all of that.

Now, I could finally live my life.

And my life included that promotion.

The interview was with Alex later this week, and I had already rehearsed it over and over in my head. Alfred could kiss my ass.

The thought of that demon made me scowl.

"What's wrong, little one?" a smooth voice said.

I felt a chill go up my spine as I turned, meeting the crimson eyes of Minni. It was damn near the middle of winter, but the cold didn't bother her. She still showed up to work wearing sleek pencil skirts and shirts that dipped low. Her lips were always bright red, her eyes always lined with a perfect cat eye, and her platinum hair always down in loose curls.

She was practically perfect in every way. The Mary Poppins of vampires. I didn't know if I was supposed to hate her or love her for that.

This wasn't even her job, she was just here to help, and yet— she had managed to solve more app report issues than my whole team.

There was a part of me that worried she would decide she wanted to work here and apply for team leader.

"Nothing," I said, setting my bag down on my desk.

Minni came over, stepping up behind me. "Allow me," she said, her voice a soft purr.

I felt a little wave of heat creep over my cheeks as she pulled off my coat, her presence alone making my pussy throb.

She knew what she was doing. We'd been dancing around each other for three weeks now. Every morning, she would come up to me. She would help me with my coat or give me a cup of coffee that was always beyond perfect. One morning I had skipped breakfast by accident, only to come to my desk to find my exact cafe order waiting for me.

"Good morning," I said, turning around to look up at her.

Her red lips tugged into a fanged smile.

Inferna was known to be a sexy boss, but then there was Minni— who was almost equally as terrifying. I wasn't sure how far the two went back, but goddess help anyone who ever got in their way.

"How are you, little flame?" she asked.

She always used a new pet name. Every morning, it was something new.

It was borderline harassment, but I couldn't stop the way it turned me on.

How in the hell was I supposed to get a promotion when I wanted to bang our office security?

It was a game. I was a mouse, and she was the cat that had me pinned down.

"I'm okay," I sighed. "I'm just figuring out living situation things."

"Makes sense," Minni said. "Although, Cinder has a right to worry."

I shot her a sour look, but I didn't have it in me to glare. "Not you too."

She shrugged. "You can hate it all you want. It doesn't

change the truth, love bug. They love you and care for you. I'll see you later. I need to attend to some things."

I nodded and watched as she went, barely doing anything to hide the fact that I was staring at her ass.

"Why don't you ask her out already?"

I looked up at Jaehan as he set his things down on his desk. His hair was damp, and there was a sucker mark on his cheek from a tentacle.

I raised a brow, but he only grinned.

The office was buzzing around us, monsters and witches coming in from the cold. The skies were gray outside, and snow not too far away.

That was one of my favorite things about this office. I liked to watch the weather change throughout the day.

"Shut up," I sighed. "It's not like that."

Jaehan rolled his eyes as he took his seat. "Sure, Ember. Sure. I think I remember saying that too..."

"Shut up," I hissed. "Everyone is on my ass this morning. It's annoying."

I started up my computer, taking my seat.

Jaehan chuckled, starting up his computer too. He leaned forward, his mouse clicking rapidly.

"Oh, hell. Ember, we have a meeting in twenty minutes," Jaehan said, letting out a long sigh. "Our whole team does."

Recently, Alex and Inferna made the decision to split the office into pods for easier management– which was also why the position for team leader had opened up. I had ended up in the Mugroot group, and our team was performing well despite the barriers between the rest of the team.

The two monsters and witches on our team liked to keep to themselves. Jaehan and I were convinced it was because we were omegas and potentially because Billy had already threatened to slit anyone's throat who pissed off his mate.

It would be something I would need to be able to work on if I became team leader.

I took a deep breath, trying not to focus on that too much. I had a tendency to hyperfocus on certain things, and team leader was what had been haunting me.

We spent the next few minutes checking emails and then finally grabbed our laptops, heading to one of the conference rooms.

"I'll be there in a minute," Jaehan said.

I sighed dramatically, watching as he went toward his two monster mates. I lingered for a moment as they both turned their undivided attention on him, Billy and Charlie grinning like fools.

Monsters who were simps for their mates were adorable.

I went down the hall, ignoring some of the heads that turned to watch me pass.

I wasn't the only omega in the office, and yet I sometimes felt like I was the one who was scrutinized the most. Part of me wanted to say it was just paranoia, but I'd seen the looks. The hungry ones.

So long as I stayed away from a heat cycle, I would be fine. Those were the fucking worst, anyway.

"Good morning," Inferna chimed as I stepped into the conference room.

"Hi," I said, giving her a quick smile.

She was rifling through papers while Art was typing notes on his laptop, his brows pulled into a scowl. Those two were a power couple, and then with Calen in the mix, they became a dynamic trio that I envied.

Fuck. I needed to do something with someone and get all the romance vibes out of my system.

There were moments when it hurt to see someone look at another the way Art, Inferna, and Calen looked at each other. Same for Cinder and their mates, and Jaehan and his too.

An orc woman who I had never seen before was seated to Inferna's right. She had her dark hair in a French braid, wore a black turtleneck with black high-waisted pants, and was all muscle. She was seated, but I knew the moment she stood up, she would have to be at least seven feet tall.

I stared for a moment, feeling a flutter in my stomach.

She looked up at me, her lips pulling into a slow smile. Her tusks were short and polished, gleaming in the office light.

I'd never seen an orc woman before, but she was gorgeous. A crush-you-like-a-watermelon-between-her-thighs type of gorgeous.

"I thought this was a meeting for our pod?" I asked.

"Nope," Inferna said. "Don't stress. Just take a seat. We'll be starting soon. This was going to be a meeting for the pod, but we pushed that to later. This is just a meeting for you. The calendar invite should have been updated, but you might have missed it. It's early."

My cheeks heated as I took a seat, trying to pull my attention away from her. "Is this about the interview tomorrow?"

"Nope," Inferna said. She looked up, giving me a soft smile. "Relax, Ember."

All the women in this office were hot as fuck. Everywhere I turned, there was another monster lady who was a sexy badass, and I was ready to be just like them.

"Can you close the door?" Inferna asked, looking at Art.

He nodded and stood, going to close it.

I frowned more now. I was nervous. I didn't like being in rooms alone, even with people I trusted. And it wasn't that I was alone but...

Cinder wasn't here.

The thought made me a little angry. I couldn't always rely on them, but they had become my comfort default. If Cinder was around, I was safe.

I had to break that pattern.

I was an independent woman. An independent witch. I had my own job and soon to be my own apartment.

"This is Lea," Inferna said. "She is going to be your assigned guardian."

"My what?" I asked, leaning forward in my seat.

"Your guardian," Inferna said again. Her eyes held mine, her expression unwavering. "She will be with you during office hours and will ensure that you get home safely until further notice. And before you ask, no, this wasn't Cinder's idea. This was mine. All of the omegas in the office right now are in danger, but you are especially."

"Why?" I hissed. "Why me? I haven't done anything."

"You escaped," Art said, planting his hands on the table. "And you are also the only one in the office who has used your magic against them so far. Jaehan already has his mates, so we aren't as worried. But with your history with them, we're concerned."

"Art is right," Inferna said. "And you're a smart witch, Ember. You know we're right."

I made a little noise, tearing my gaze away from them. "I thought we were over all of that. I have the interview tomorrow and our team has been doing really good."

"You hoped we were over all that. Believe me, I hoped too, but I highly doubt that we are. Also, this is a separate thing from your interview. This is just us trying to protect you, Ember," Art said.

They were right, but I didn't want this. I didn't want to be a burden again, and that's exactly what I would be to Lea.

"I'd like to talk to Ember alone," Lea said, looking up at Inferna.

"Alone?" Art asked, scowling.

Inferna was silent for a moment, her tail flicking behind her. She then nodded, grabbing her folder. "Fine. Come on, Art."

I scowled as I watched them leave. The door clicked shut, and I was left sitting across from the monster who was supposed to protect me from all the evil in the fucking world now.

She leaned forward, her eyes drawing me in. "Now listen," she said. "I know you don't want others to worry about you, but letting your ego get in the way isn't going to help you."

"I'm strong," I bit out. "My magic makes me stronger than most witches, aside from ones like Alex. I think I've proved that I can handle myself."

"True," Lea said, smiling. "You're powerful and capable of taking care of yourself. I never said you weren't. But you're also powerful enough to let someone else be there to have your back. You know, in case there is another attack or kidnapping or mind game."

"You wouldn't be able to help with that," I said. "Orcs aren't magic wielders."

She snorted. "No, but with the family I come from, we may as well be. I think you'll find I can be helpful, honey.

Plus, you mentioned an interview? If its anything for management, then the first thing you have to learn is how to delegate. Delegate your safety to me."

The southern drawl melted me just a little. I sighed, leaning back in my chair and looking up at the ceiling.

"I'm tired," I whispered. "I'm tired of fighting."

"It'll be over before you know it," she said.

"How do you know?" I said softly. "How does anyone know? This has been most of my life. When will it be over?"

Why was I saying these things to her?

Lea stood and came around the table to me, looking down. I looked up at her, my heart thrumming louder than before.

Fuck, she was really pretty. I swallowed hard, holding her gaze.

"Do you want me to be honest?" she asked.

"Yes," I said, my voice barely a whisper. Tears blurred my vision for a moment, but I reined them back in.

"It won't be over until Aamon is gone. And I don't know when that will be, but there are plans to make it happen. In the meantime, we need to keep you safe. I don't know everything about you. I don't know your history aside from what Cinder, who was very vague, shared. But I do know that having someone watching your back isn't a bad idea, and I certainly don't mind keeping an eye on a pretty little witch like you. Understood?"

My stomach did a slow flip, warmth spreading through my chest.

I couldn't tell her no, not with her looking at me like that.

"You're very convincing," I said.

"I've heard that once or twice," she chuckled.

I smiled now, relaxing. "Fine. I don't like this, though. And please don't treat me like an idiot or like I'm helpless."

"Those are the exact opposite of what I think about you, even though we just met."

Those butterflies came back, and she winked.

"Let's go get a cup of coffee from the kitchen and then maybe get some actual work done."

How in the hell was I going to focus on work now that I just agreed to let a sexy orc be my guardian?

CHAPTER TWO

heat

LEA

THE OMEGA WITCH was too cute for her own good.

I sat down at the desk across from her, looking around the office for what felt like the hundredth time. I had studied every face in this place, logging them each mentally. I took a sip of my coffee, looking for anything that felt out of place.

There were the monsters and witches who we knew were good, and then there was everyone else. Any one of them could be bad, and there was no way to tell until things started to happen again.

And we knew they would happen again. It was just a matter of when.

I was originally supposed to be here earlier but ended up taking the Griffin who had survived this whole mess and driving him up north. I'd dumped him at a hunting lodge that my dads owned, leaving him there to sort through his own shit.

I wasn't going to judge him for being on the wrong side of things. We all had times when we made mistakes, and hopefully, he would learn from his.

He was lucky Inferna had shown him mercy. Of course, her temper wasn't quite as bad as her monster father.

Part of me wished that I could be with the family at one of the other lodges, but I knew I had to be here right now. I had three other siblings, all brothers. We had been adopted from an early age and were very loved.

I was happy to be an Orc. Bonds carried the same weight as blood, and I'd never felt out of place. I had been raised to be compassionate, to work hard, and to do what I loved.

Having one human dad made for some fun family photos, that was for sure.

I let out a sigh, glancing around again. I didn't trust more than half this office, and now I was in charge of keeping the pretty omega safe.

There was something about her. I had seen her before she'd seen me, and I had felt a tug in my heart.

It was too soon to let myself feel for anyone else. After everything that had happened with Minni, time being a single lady was needed.

But then again...

I looked back at Ember. She had pulled her purple hair up into a bun now and was already working, using the reports as a way to not think about everything happening.

I wanted her.

The stark thought jolted through me, and I damn near cursed aloud.

I couldn't think about that. I couldn't think about her doing anything with me.

But hell, I'd sure enjoyed looking down into her eyes. I could have stayed there all day, just taking in every line and curve of her face. Studying all the little freckles or the way her eyes gave away what she was thinking.

"You're staring at me," Ember said, her tone flat but with a smile creeping over her face.

"Not staring. Just watching," I said. "Making sure the boogeyman doesn't pull any shit."

She grinned, typing away on her computer.

There were so many desks in the place, and all I could think about was hoisting her up onto one, making her lie back, and helping her forget about all her troubles for a while.

I could feel a gaze locked on me, and I looked up, not surprised to see my vampire ex stalking toward us.

"For fuck's sake," I sighed.

"What?" Ember asked, looking around.

She froze, watching Minni as she walked up.

"We need to talk," Minni said, planting her hand on the back of Ember's chair. "You and me, Lea."

"I'm working," I said.

"Is there something wrong?" Ember asked.

"Yes," Minni hissed. Her eyes were crimson daggers pointed at me, and I knew she was ready to dice me up.

"I can't leave Ember," I said, taking another sip of my coffee. "And whatever you want to say, I'm sure it can wait until we're off the clock."

"No," Minni said. "I want to talk to you now. *Now.*"

A little bolt of anger worked through me, but I kept it down. I leaned forward in my seat, holding the vampire's gaze. "No."

Her perfect face flickered with a deadly look, her eyes darkening.

"Hey," Ember said, her voice strained.

I looked at her and fought off a frown. Her eyes were wide, and a deep blush had crept over her. I raised a brow, catching her scent.

For a moment, I wondered if she'd just gone into heat, but then it quickly passed.

Minni had also stilled, her gaze locked on the witch.

"Are you okay, sweetheart?"

I immediately glared at Minni. Seriously??

"Fuck off Minni," I said under my breath.

"I'm okay," Ember said, nodding. "Uh... I'm going to go to the restroom."

She stood up, and so did I. She paused, looking at me.

"You don't need to go with me to pee."

"Someone has to stay with you," I said. "Remember. Boogeyman."

She shook her head, moving past Minni and heading toward the restrooms.

I followed after her, only for Minni to catch me by my arm and stop me.

"What?!" I snarled under my breath, looking down at her.

"The witch is mine, Lea," she hissed. "*Mine*. She belongs to me. I should have been the one to protect her."

"Well, Inferna chose me," I said. "So take that up with her. And fuck right off."

Minni started to argue, but I yanked away, ignoring her growl as I followed Ember.

Things were already weird enough, but the fact that Minni was so possessive over the witch pissed me off.

There had been a time when hearing such a thing

would have made me smile. Neither one of us had ever wanted to be with just one person while we were dating, so there had been times in our relationship when we'd also dated others separately. There was a nice warm and fuzzy feeling when I knew she was out with someone who made her happy, and vice versa.

But that fuzzy feeling was gone.

I wanted Ember. I felt the streak of possessiveness, the lure of lust. Hell, I'd just met her, but I always trusted my gut.

I went down the hall, pushing open the restroom door. I heard a low moan and froze.

Fuck.

Her scent hit me first. The one I had thought I imagined only moments ago.

Desire curled through me. The need to *mate*. To fuck.

I took a deep breath, walking down to the last stall. The door was open, and Ember was sitting on the floor, her head between her knees.

"Ember," I said, keeping my voice soft. "Let me take you home."

She shook her head, her shoulders trembling.

Even through the lust, I felt a pang of worry.

I took another deep breath, trying to control myself. To focus on her needs.

I knelt down next to her, putting my hand gently on her shoulder.

She looked up, her eyes locking with mine. Tears ran down her cheeks, the look of terror making me wish I could hunt down any fucker who had ever hurt her.

"Hey," I whispered. "It's okay, love. I'm not going to hurt you. I am going to get you out of the office, though."

"I shouldn't be in heat," she said, her bottom lip quivering. "This shouldn't be happening, but it is, and I don't know what to do. My cycle shouldn't be here for another couple of months."

I felt the tug again, stronger. Fiercer. I watched her for a moment, trying not to think about the things I wanted to do to her.

"We'll figure it out," I said. "But for right now, let me get you home. Okay?"

Ember nodded, and I offered my hand. She took it, and I pulled her to standing, only to catch her as she stumbled forward.

Ah, fuck. A little bird, a little witch. I held on to her for a moment.

The gods would have to grant me strength because getting her home safe was going to be a pain in the ass.

"Alright," I said. "Let's get to the elevator. I will let the boss know later. We just need to get you home."

CHAPTER THREE
little lady

MINNI

I GLARED as my ex walked my witch across the office, the two of them moving swiftly. Heads turned as they passed, and a couple of growls echoed through the office.

That witch was *mine* — but Inferna had insisted that Lea be the one to guard her.

Inferna was lucky we both loved her because being in the office with *her* was already torture. I was trying to move on, for fuck's sake.

They went towards the elevators, and I found myself moving toward them.

I wasn't letting the two of them out of my sight. I didn't care if it made me look like a bitch. I didn't care if I was turning heads as I marched their way.

Ember needed to be with me.

I went out into the hall and slid through the doors behind the two of them.

"Minni," Lea growled. "Go away. I'm taking her home. Go back to work."

Ember backed up into the corner of the elevator, her eyes widening. The doors slid shut behind me, putting the three of us together.

"I *am* working," I said. "Making sure that Ember is safe."

"She *is* safe," Lea said, her surprise turning into a disgruntled glare. "She's with me. I'm her guardian."

"Well, so am I," I said. "I've been watching her a lot longer than you have. Plus, I doubt you'll be able to keep up with her."

"What the fuck is that supposed to mean?" she snarled.

The elevator groaned around us, and I stopped, looking up and around.

"Did you hit a button?" Lea asked.

"No," I said, turning to look at all of the buttons.

The lights flickered, drawing a gasp from Ember, and then went out.

"Oh shit," I said.

"What the fuck?" Lea growled.

I felt Ember's fear and looked at her. I could see her in the dark, her eyes shut.

"Hey," I said, dropping my voice into a seductive tone. It was one I had used for centuries to lure my prey in, but... now I was using it to calm her. "It's okay. The power will come back on. The storm coming in probably knocked out some power lines."

Lea gave me a wary look. The two of us silently called a truce for the moment.

"I don't like the dark," Ember whispered.

"You can use your magic," Lea said.

Ember nodded and held out her hand.

Witches had always been a wonder to me. I watched as

light bloomed in her palm, a golden hue washing over the three of us.

And then I caught her scent.

Fuck.

Thirst unlike anything I had felt in centuries washed over me, making me back up against the opposite wall. Lea growled, immediately stepping between us.

Shit.

"This is why I told you to go back," Lea said. "She's gone into heat."

"Why didn't you fucking say so?" I hissed, my fangs already lengthening. It was involuntary, the primal part of me aching to be set free.

All because she smelled like she was ready for me to take her. To taste her, to make her forget about everything around us.

I took a deep breath, letting out a soft growl. A hungry one. I could hear Ember's heart beating, her scent growing stronger.

"Fuck," Ember whispered. "Fuck. FUCK."

"What's happening?" Lea asked.

"It's getting worse," Ember whimpered. "I feel like I'm melting."

Lea looked at her, back at me, and then at the elevator doors. "We'll get you out of here. Minni is a pain, but she can help."

"I don't know why I'd suddenly go into heat like this. It doesn't make any sense. I don't have another cycle planned, at least for another couple of months. I feel like my entire body is catching on fire and—"

Ember continued to ramble, her scent becoming stronger and stronger the longer we stood here. I closed my eyes, trying not to focus on her, but it was impossible.

My throat burned. My fangs ached, desperate to bury into her neck.

Not to mention the arousal.

Her scent was becoming headier, dripping with need. She needed me to take care of her, needed me to pin her against the wall and take her.

"Minni," Lea said, the only voice of reason. She stepped closer to me, grabbing me by the shoulders. "Control yourself, woman. You have to. We're stuck in an elevator, and we have to protect her. Not devour her."

I looked up at her, wanting to glare. Wanting to hate her.

It was at moments like this that I remembered why I had loved her in the first place.

Lea's eyes softened, and she turned, looking back at the witch.

At the *omega*.

Ember let out a soft moan. Her magic had died, leaving the three of us in the dark elevator. I watched as she looked at us, her eyes searching.

I then watched as her hand slid down to her pussy.

I wanted to taste her. I needed to taste her, to have her essence coat my tongue and lips. I wanted to leave a trail of red lipstick stains from her collarbone, down her breasts and stomach, to her clit.

"I'm sorry," Ember whispered. "This one is really bad."

"Let me help you," I said, not even caring that Lea was here.

"Minni," Lea hissed.

"Let me help," I said again. "At least until the elevator starts, and we can get you out of here."

"You can't help her right now," Lea growled. "You'd fucking drink her blood from her clit like this."

The thought of her blood made me groan. I covered my mouth and looked away, glaring at Lea. "Fuck you. I have more control than that."

Lea snorted and then stepped forward. "Do you?"

"Do *you?*" I hissed, watching as Ember moved closer to her.

"No," Lea said. "No, I don't. Ember, what do you want from us right now?"

"I want to cum," she whispered, her voice desperate. "I need to. I don't care how. I just need to."

"If we do this, we will take you home after."

"Home where?"

"To my place," I said. "To my home. Away from the office."

"I have to work tomorrow," she said.

"Not like this," Lea snorted.

Ember ignored her words and stepped forward, surprising the two of us as she leaned up on her tiptoes and kissed my Orc ex.

Lea was shocked, but then I watched as she melted.

Fucking hell. I had missed her.

This was turning into a cluster fuck.

A soft moan left the two of them, and Ember wrapped her arms around Lea, only for Lea to lift her and push her against the wall.

My blood roared as I watched them, aroused by the sight. By the scents of their need, by the sounds they each made as they devoured each other.

My pussy pulsed and I groaned, covering my mouth with my palm for a moment. My fangs throbbed in the same rhythm, aching for something different.

Lea groaned and set her down, breaking their kiss with a heavy gasp.

"Fuck. Fuck, we have to get out."

Ember pushed the straps of her jumpsuit to the side, the loops falling down to her waist.

"Ember," I said, my voice almost pleading. "I won't be able to stop if you keep going."

"I said I want to cum," Ember said, looking up at me. "Are you going to help me with that or not? Because if not, then you can just watch us."

I raised a brow, my lips parting.

I was about to lunge toward her, but the lights flickered above us. We all looked up, watching as they came back on and the elevator came to life.

Lea leaned past me and hit the button for the first floor, giving me a dark look. "I think Inferna will understand."

"Agreed," I said, looking back at Ember.

"Not fair," she moaned.

"Be patient," I said. "We'll get you home, and then I'll show you how good girls that are patient get rewarded."

"You can try," she quipped. "Maybe you should try feeling like your body is burning up from the inside out."

The elevator slowed as it hit the first floor, the doors sliding open. Ember started to move past us, but Lea caught her, hoisting her up over her shoulders. I had the perfect view of her ass in that jumpsuit now. She let out a squeal, trying to kick free, but I watched with a satisfied smirk as my ex carted her across the parking garage.

Lea already knew we were taking my car, going to my black Porsche SUV. I pulled my keys out, and the doors automatically unlocked.

I half expected her to make a comment about it like she used to, but instead, she opened the back door and shoved our omega inside. *Who in the hell gets a Porsche SUV? Why not a regular Porsche?*

I went to the driver's seat, climbed in, and slammed the door.

Ember let out a pained moan, and I shook my head, turning on the AC to full blast despite the fact that it was cold for them. I couldn't feel the sting of the temperature, but I knew the air would at least push her scent away so I could focus on driving.

"Trying to freeze us?" Lea asked as I pulled out of the parking spot and raced through the garage.

Driving was one of my favorite things. I liked to test my reflexes, which Lea hated.

"Trying to kill us?" she asked as I shot out onto the road, cutting off a couple of other drivers.

I ignored her, looking back at our omega.

OUR OMEGA?

Fuck no. I glared, flooring the gas. Fuck no. I was not going to think of her as ours.

"Trying to—"

"Lea," I snarled. "Focus on her, please."

Lea sighed and looked back at Ember.

Ember let out a long moan, followed by the sort of whimper I would be hearing soon.

I knew what had been happening in this office, but I was trying not to think about that. I was trying not to think about why her heat would have been triggered now.

If she were my mate alone, it would have happened before.

But, if she was meant to be both of ours...

And that was what had caused this...

"Where are we going?" Ember moaned.

"Home," I said. "To my home, where only a demon who wants to end up back in hell would dare trespass."

"I want you," Ember said. "Both of you. It's not fair."

"What isn't fair?" Lea asked. "You've got us both, sweetheart."

"It's not fair because I didn't want this. I didn't want to be a burden again."

"You're not a burden," Lea and I said in unison.

I gave Ember an uneasy look as I swerved through traffic. I made it to the highway and floored it, speeding towards my home.

"We'll be there in twenty," I said. "Just sit back and close your eyes."

"I need to cum."

"Then cum," I said, glancing at her through the rearview.

Ember held my gaze for a moment and then, to my delight, started to strip out of her clothes.

Lea let out a soft growl, now completely twisted in her seat.

"If you make her cum," I said, looking at Lea, "I want a taste."

Lea shook her head but didn't say no, focusing back on Ember.

"You're so pretty," Lea sighed.

I stole another look through the rearview right as Ember slid out of her panties, tossing them to the side.

"Don't wreck us," Lea muttered to me.

It would be a challenge not to.

The sound of my phone ringing echoed through the car, but I ignored it, drowning it out as I focused on the rush of Ember's blood. The sound of her heart pounding, the scent of her need. Of her slick.

Lea cursed. "Eyes on me, little lady."

I smiled, enjoying the familiar phrase. In the bedroom, the two of us had always had a very fun switch dynamic.

There had been times I would lead, others when she would. Sometimes I would tie her up, other times she would leave me cuffed to the bed all day and periodically come check on me and make me cum over and over again.

Fuck, those had been good days.

"Spread your legs for me," Lea said.

Ember let out a low whimper. "I want you," she whispered. "I want both of you. I've wanted both of you since I saw you, but this is...."

"Different," Lea finished. "We'll figure it out, but I thought you wanted to cum? Why are you still worrying when your legs are spread, and your pussy is begging for attention?"

Ember made a noise that made me smile.

I couldn't wait to taste her blood. Well...If she would let me.

I hoped that she would.

"We're getting closer," I said.

"Touch yourself," Lea said. "I want to see how you like it, and then when we get home, we can see if I do it well."

"Yes," Ember gasped. "Ah, please."

The little beg made me suck in a breath, and I shifted in my seat, wishing I could switch places with Lea. It was torture to listen to her start to rub herself, knowing she was wet and ready.

"Good girl," Lea said softly, her voice husky. "You look good like this, you know. Your fingers in your pussy and a beg on your lips."

Ember started to rub faster, and I let out a growl, stealing glances every moment I could.

She was in the middle of the back seat, her legs spread with an expression of ecstasy on her face.

"Faster," Lea commanded.

"Yes," Ember groaned. "Fuck."

I had been courting her for three weeks, and all of the seductive and sexy vibes I had given just melted into an impatient need to get her home and breed her like a little slut.

"Little flame," I said, my voice melodic. "Are you going to cum for us? Without us even touching you?"

I heard Lea's breath hitch and couldn't hide my victorious smile.

She still felt things for me too.

Damn it. All of my thoughts were either about Ember or about winning Lea back.

Would I even be able to?

The way our relationship had ended hadn't been the best.

"Yes," Ember gasped. "I'm so close."

I listened to the sounds and reached out, turning off the AC. Her scent immediately washed over me, making my mouth water.

My driveway was close now.

"Eyes on me," Lea said again.

"Watch her, little flame," I said. "She's going to devour you soon. Make you feel things you've never felt before."

Ember let out a sharp cry. I gripped the steering wheel as she came, a soft growl leaving me as she panted and moaned.

"Taste," I said, giving Lea a dark look.

Lea let out a short sigh and then leaned back. "May I?"

"Yes," Ember groaned. "Ah fuck, your fingers feel good."

I glanced back, unable to stop myself. I watched Lea's fingers for a split moment before looking back at the road, wishing that Lea was in my seat and I was in hers.

"I know," Lea chuckled, leaning back and offering me the fingers that had just dipped inside our omega.

I looked at her now, letting my instincts take over the drive as I parted my lips.

Lea didn't hesitate even though I had fangs. Even though I could bite her and drain her.

The taste of Ember burst on my tongue, and I groaned, enjoying it. Lea pulled her fingers free and then licked them, arching a brow.

I turned onto my driveway, taking us to the front of my house. It was on the outskirts of the city, one of the many houses I had on standby in case I needed a place to stay.

The tires screeched as I slammed on the brakes, the door already opening as I jumped out. Snow fell on me, sticking to my clothing as I yanked open the back door.

Lea pulled open the other side, our gazes locking.

Ember looked at her and then at me.

"Who's carrying you?" Lea asked.

"Uh, I don't think anyone should, and I'm still naked—"

"Nonsense," I said, leaning in.

I pulled Ember towards me, enjoying her yelp of surprise at my strength. Like I wasn't a fucking ancient vampire. I could kick a car and send the bitch rolling.

Was I doing this because Lea had already carried her? *Maybe.*

Ember let out another yelp as I picked her up and then took her to the door, my speed leaving her breathless. I heard Lea's wry chuckle.

Was I showing off?

Yes.

"I'm naked," Ember gasped.

"Well, good thing my neighbors know better than to look this way," I said, stepping into my home.

She held on to me, her little whimper making me smile. She was warm and her soft skin smelled like jasmine. I was painfully aware of the fact that she was naked and enjoying every single moment of it.

"God, your home is gorgeous," she said.

"Well, I like pretty things," I said, looking down at her.

Her eyes widened a little, that blush creeping back. It was cute.

She was cute.

Gods damn it, we were fucked.

"I have a shower upstairs, along with a tub," I said. "We'll draw you a bubble bath. And then we can see about other things."

"Okay," she said.

Lea stepped inside behind me, shutting the door and cutting off the cold. The world outside was a snowy one, but indoors it was warm and inviting.

Perfect for making a nest together. Perfect for breaking her heat.

I let Ember down, and Lea wrapped her coat around her.

"Upstairs," I said, nodding towards them. "Help yourself to bath bombs and salts, or whatever you'd like. I need to have a word with your *guardian*."

CHAPTER FOUR

fangs and tusks

EMBER

THE HEAT of the water felt good on my muscles, drawing another little groan from me. The bathtub was massive and gorgeous, black porcelain with gold accents and clawed feet. All of the tile in the bathroom was gray with veins of gold too.

My vampire co-worker had a very elegant gothic style, one that was evocative. It was regal, expensive, and pretty.

What the fuck was I doing?

The thought struck me for a moment, a voice of clarity in the cloud that had overcome me.

Once the two of them had been around me together, I hadn't been able to stop it. I had gone into heat, which only meant one thing.

Minni and Lea were my mates.

Fuck. I hadn't wanted this. I hadn't wanted to be tied down. I didn't want the two of them to feel like they had to care for me. The way they both looked at me...

My stomach gave a hard tug. I looked up, catching my reflection in a mirror with a filigree frame.

God, Minni's home was wild.

I looked like I was running a fever, and my skin was giving a soft golden glow. My purple hair was still tied back, the loose strands now wet from the water.

I felt out of place in this type of space, but I liked it.

In fact, I liked both Lea and Minni too.

Even though I didn't want this.

I struggled with the thoughts, going back and forth. Lea had held my gaze as I had cum in the car. *In the backseat of a vampire's car.* All because the need for a release had been so fucking strong, so unbearable.

Lea with her dark green skin and her honey-brown eyes. I wondered how those tusks would feel against my pussy as she ate me out.

And Minni.

I thought about her fangs and sucked in a breath.

I had been trapped for the last few years, unable to escape all of the monsters who had been out to get me. I had very rarely been able to escape to have sex with anyone, and whenever I had, it hadn't been memorable.

But her fangs would be memorable.

Was *this* crazy? Was *I* crazy?

Yes, and *yes*.

But I couldn't talk myself out of it. I wanted both of them. I wanted to be with them, even if I didn't end up as their mate.

I heard the sound of footsteps and looked up as Lea came into the doorway.

"Hi," she said, freezing where she stood.

"Hi." My voice was a soft whisper.

"I let Inferna know we stole you," Lea said, her shoulders relaxing as she stepped into the bathroom. "And she let Cinder know you're safe."

I nodded, feeling a sense of relief.

I didn't want Cinder worrying about me anymore.

"Thank you," I said.

"How are you feeling?"

"Okay," I said, giving her a weak smile. "Still very much turned on and wanting to do *things*. Are you and Minni okay?"

"We're exes."

Oh. Oh fuck.

"Before you say anything, just listen," Lea said. "We've been broken up for a couple of months, and we ended things because we were having a difficult time keeping up with our lives and each other. It wasn't necessarily because we stopped wanting each other, but... it had just changed, and we didn't know why. We loved each other but ended up breaking it off."

"You didn't have to explain," I said, frowning. "I don't want you to feel like you have to tell me your business."

"We wanted to because, at the moment, it affects you," Lea said. "And we agreed that we would be honest with you. Obviously, you didn't go into heat with just her or just me. You did with both of us."

That was true.

"And I know this is a sudden change."

I felt a little prick in my heart, looking away. "Just because I'm in heat doesn't mean that either one of you has to commit to me. You don't have to be with me forever."

Lea hummed, coming to the edge of the tub. She knelt down, tipping my face up. I met her gaze, warm and sweet like honey. The way I'd always dreamed someone would look at me.

"Making this decision while you are in heat might be a little rash, but... nothing is holding me here right now, Ember. I could walk away if I wanted, even though it would be hard. But I want to stay here with you. Are you worried we're going to force you to become our mate? Or that I would do that?"

"No," I said, swallowing hard. "No. I know you wouldn't unless I wanted to."

Lea held me for a few moments, leaning in closer. I felt my pussy flutter, my eyes falling to her tusks and lips.

She smiled and let go of me with a rattled breath. "Minni is cooking. She's a good cook, despite the fact that she drinks blood."

"Where does she get her blood?" I asked, sitting up. The water sloshed around as I moved onto my knees.

At some point in my life, I had become really comfortable being naked, and right now was no exception. I fought off the urge to smile as Lea made another noise, her gaze fighting to stay on mine and not slide down to my body. I owned every single curve I had, every roll and soft line.

"Vampires have their resources. Most of them come from blood banks. People donate to hospitals and for vampires without realizing it." She blew out a breath. "Woman, you're really testing me right now."

"Maybe," I said with a provocative grin. "I've never actually been with anyone while in heat. Usually, I'd just lock myself in my room, and Cinder would leave food at my door."

Lea frowned. "That sounds...terrible."

"They did their best," I said. "And I appreciate everything. But, I guess I've decided that even though I don't know how I feel about relationships right now, sex isn't off the table."

She arched a brow. "Oh yeah?"

"Yeah," I said, standing up. Water dripped down my body, gleaming like tiny diamonds over my glorious curves. At this point, I accepted the fact that I was going to give off a soft glow until my heat broke.

However long that would take.

"If you want."

"I do want," Lea said. She blew out a whistle and then went to a cabinet in the corner of the bathroom, coming back with a very soft cobalt blue towel. "Step out, princess."

I couldn't help but smile. I stepped out of the bath, immediately wrapped in the warmth of the towel. Lea leaned down, pressing a kiss against the curve of my neck as she started to dry me off.

Her hands roamed over me, swiping up every drop of water. I breathed in her scent, closing my eyes as she touched me.

"Lea," I whispered.

She lowered herself in front of me, taking the towel with her. I let out a breath as she parted my legs.

"May I?" she asked, looking up at me.

"Yes," I breathed, my pussy pulsing with need.

She nodded and leaned forward, licking up any stray drops of water. She kissed from my lower stomach, down my thighs. My head tipped back as she sent shivers through me.

"You taste like heaven, little lady," she whispered, parting my legs further.

I sucked in a breath just as the tip of her tongue lapped at my clit. I let out a long groan, my hands reaching out and gripping her head. My fingers curled into her hair as she began to lap at me.

The towel dropped to the floor, and she ran her fingers up my inner thighs, bringing them to my pussy. She spread my lips, her tusks rubbing against me as her tongue pushed inside of me.

I let out a sharp cry, my hips bucking with need. I felt like my bones had melted, my blood rushing as pleasure rolled through me.

I was going to cum again, this time on her tongue.

She let out a low growl, her arms sweeping beneath my thighs. I squealed as I was lifted in one swift motion, my legs draping over her shoulders as she picked me up. She held my pussy to her face, her tongue thrusting in and out of me as she carried me to the bed in the room that joined the bathroom.

I gasped as she spread me back, forcing my legs wide so she could fuck me harder with her tongue.

I gripped the blankets, my hips thrusting in the same rhythm as she drove me wild. I cried out, succumbing to the primal need.

I heard a low growl, one that had my eyes flying open. I looked at the doorway as Minni stepped in, her crimson eyes feasting on the two of us.

My eyes fluttered as Lea's tusks rubbed against me, her tongue doing things that only a devil should be able to do. Minni's soft laugh filled the room as she came to the edge of the bed.

I found myself reaching out and pulling her down, our lips meeting.

A low purr left her, and I gasped as Minni pushed me into the mattress, pinning my hands above my head.

"Look at you," she said, baring her fangs. "You want monsters, sweetheart?"

"Yes," I gasped. "Please— ah!" I cried out as Lea drove

me closer to the edge, all of my thoughts becoming jumbled.

Minni grinned and leaned in, kissing down my neck and chest. I was making all sorts of noises now, my entire body on fire as I felt her sharp fangs over one of my nipples.

"Please," I begged, panting.

"You want me to bite you?"

"Yes," I cried. "Fuck!"

She didn't hesitate, taking my breast into her mouth and biting. I cried out, the pain and pleasure giving me the best orgasm I'd ever had. It slammed into me as Lea held me still. I came on her tongue with a cry as Minni fed from my breasts.

My head was spinning, and I closed my eyes, every thought evaporating. I couldn't think straight, couldn't see straight. Someone could tell me aliens were real right now, and I'd just smile and wave, not knowing what planet I was on.

Lea groaned, slowly pulling away. I could feel Minni taking more of my blood until she slowly let go, her fangs pulling free.

I opened my eyes as she swiped her tongue over the bite marks, lapping up the drops of blood.

My lips parted to speak, but instead, I made a noise that had both of them giggling.

"You're very cute," Minni said. "And very needy."

I nodded, making a satisfied hum. Lea crawled up on the bed next to me, and I leaned up, giving her a kiss. She smiled, cupping my face for a moment before pressing her forehead to mine.

The tenderness made tears spring up, blurring my vision.

Was this what I had been missing? This type of care and sweetness?

"I made some soup with some braided French bread," Minni said, sitting up. She let go of my hands, giving me a sweet but wicked smile. "Ready for dinner?"

"Yes," I sighed happily.

"Dinner and more sex," Lea teased.

I grinned.

Maybe being stuck with a vampire and orc during this heat wouldn't be so bad after all.

CHAPTER FIVE
dinner

LEA

I HAD MISSED Minni's cooking, which made me a little sad and a little happy at the same time.

The three of us had eaten dinner and spent an hour talking about random things. There were moments when Ember struggled to focus, when her scent would become almost intoxicating, but then it would pass.

I had never met a witch who went into heat. I'd run across certain monsters that did, but I'd never experienced it firsthand like this.

Ember was captivating. She was gorgeous, smart and creative. She told me that during the times she had to stay out of the way of evil creatures after her, she'd spent it drawing and painting beautiful works of art.

I didn't know Cinder, but I respected the fact that they had done everything to protect her.

There was something about her. We were in the middle

of winter, but talking to her was like running through a field in the spring.

From what I had heard about her magic, that seemed to be how she was.

Bright, energetic, lovely and creative.

"You have that look," Minni murmured as I cleaned off the dishes.

She'd sent Ember to the living room with a glass of wine, leaving the two of us alone for a moment.

"What look?" I asked, looking down at her.

She smiled, leaning against the counter. Her eyes were a bright red since she had tasted Ember's blood, her crimson lipstick not out of place. She was still wearing her work clothes, which meant from this angle, I had a perfect view down her blouse.

"That look," Minni said. "The falling in love one. But you've just met her."

"And you?" I asked. "You've been stalking her for weeks."

Minni scoffed, but she didn't disagree. "Stalking is archaic. Courting is my preference."

"Sure," I said, smirking. "Just like you courted me."

I hadn't meant to say that, but now the words hung heavily between us. Minni looked away, her expression becoming unreadable.

"I've missed you," she whispered. "I didn't want to end our relationship. We were trying to do what was best, but I've just become a bitter dead thing again."

"I don't even know why we broke up," I said.

"Because we stopped knowing why we were together," she answered.

I made a face, but it was true.

"I've missed you too," I said. "I don't know what we're

going to do about her. She's our mate. I can feel it, the need to bond with her. To make it something more."

"To do the thing we never wanted to do," Minni said, shaking her head. "I agree, though. I can feel it too."

"I don't like this fate bullshit," I sighed, placing the last dish to the side. "'But... I know it can work out. Hell, my dads are a good example of that."

Minni immediately grinned. "That's true. And they still fuck all the time."

"Shut up," I hissed. "I do not want to think about that."

"Your dads are kind of hot—"

"Minni," I hissed again, making her snicker.

"So," she said, arching a brow. "An official truce then. We can explore whatever this is with Ember while keeping her safe from those bastards."

"Yes," I said. I couldn't keep my scowl away. "Inferna said she would be the most likely to be targeted due to her magic."

"Her magic and the fact that she killed that demon."

"What demon?" I asked.

"The fear one," Minni said. "I'm pretty sure she is the one who killed it."

We were both silent for a moment.

"Her magic is strong," Minni said. "There's a reason they would go after her again."

"They won't get to her," I said, my voice firm.

"No. They'd have to go through me first. And my family."

My family was a force to be reckoned with, but so was hers. Minni's family were all vampires, created by the same sire, who had been dead for a few years now. He had lived to a ripe old age of 9,881 and had been one of the good ones.

Her clan was one of the few vampire groups who had managed not to do anything horrendous. There were slip-ups here and there, murders of humans or monsters, but for the most part— all twenty of them were well adjusted to the world.

And even though they didn't see each other very often, one text and they would be on Minni's doorstep in a heartbeat.

My family was the same.

"They'll have orcs and vampires to get through," I said.

She nodded. "Well, I guess that says a lot about what we're feeling right now."

I smiled, finding the thought comforting.

"I'm going to go check on her," Minni said.

"Okay," I said. "I'll be along shortly."

Minni nodded and was about to walk away, but then stood up on her tiptoes and kissed my cheek.

A thousand funny feelings spread through me as she walked away, leaving me standing there a little dumb-founded.

After the two of us had broken up, it had always felt like she was the one that got away.

The idea of being back together made me happy.

The idea of being with Ember also made me happy.

What didn't make me happy was the fact that we were all in danger until further notice. Every single omega who had gone into heat recently had ended up in trouble, and in Cinder's case— that whole situation was just a mess.

Alfred was out for us. And if he wasn't right now at this very moment, then he would be soon.

It was just a matter of time.

I had done some digging into his history and had even made a few phone calls. I ended up using resources outside of the family because Inferna was trying to keep this mess away from everyone.

We could handle this. Right?

I let out a sigh, closing my eyes for a moment and trying to let the stress melt away.

I was worried about someone I'd just met. Worried about them enough to be willing to put my life at risk. Worried enough to completely ditch all plans I had this week just to protect them. Just to make sure they would be okay.

They deserved that, though. I wasn't sure what their life had been like, but the pieces I had gathered here and there told me it had been hard.

I wanted to believe that Minni and I would be able to show her life could be better. That it could be fun.

This was going to be a lot messier than I could have imagined now that emotions were involved.

Gods damn it, Minni was right, though.

I fell hard. I fell fast.

Ember made me feel things I couldn't hold down.

I opened my eyes just as a head poked through the doorway, Ember giving me a little smile. "Hey. Are you joining us? Minni has threatened to eat me if you don't."

I snorted and crossed the kitchen. "Of course. I can't let her do such a thing alone, little lady."

Ember beamed. After cumming and having a meal, you'd think that everything was right in the world.

That made me happy.

Ember lingered against the doorway, and I stepped closer to her, tipping her face up. She sucked in a breath, and I couldn't help but smile as her cheeks flushed.

"Cute," I whispered, my voice lowering. "How are you feeling?"

Her lips parted, her eyes softening. She leaned up, pulling me down into a kiss.

I grunted, wrapping my arms around her waist and lifting her. Her legs came around mine, and I pinned her against the wall, feeling the heat of her pussy through the fabric of our clothes.

Fuck. All thoughts about the demon and the office flew out of my head, replaced by how much I needed to taste her again.

Our tongues met, our kiss desperate and hungry. Her skin was soft, her scent now edged with Minni's scent too.

I broke the kiss, a low growl rumbling from my chest.

"I want you again," she whispered.

"Not until we discuss what we like," I said, setting her down gently.

Ember grinned. "Minni said the same thing."

I snorted, turning her around and pushing her toward the living room. We both walked in and were met with a very beautiful and very naked Minni lounging on her midnight blue velvet chaise.

"Fuck," we both whispered.

Her skin was smooth and radiated a warm glow from the lamps in the room, her platinum blonde curls gleaming. Her crimson lips were parted, the tips of her fangs peeking at us.

Ember let out a soft whimper. "I leave for two seconds and come back, and you're naked."

Minni smirked. "Indeed. Both of you come and sit so we can discuss."

I went to the sofa across from the chaise and took a seat, propping my ankle up on my knee. Ember sat next to me on the edge of the cushion, her eyes on Minni.

It was hard not to stare either, and I was doing my best not to look at her even though I wanted to.

Trying to prove that I still had self-control.

That me wanting her was a choice.

"I have specific tastes," Minni said. "Things that I enjoy. And if you are interested in some of those things, I would love to do them with you. With both of you, although I won't sign Lea up without her saying she wants to."

"What kind of tastes?" Ember whispered.

"The carnal kind," Minni purred.

Fuck it.

I looked over at her, my eyes roaming over her. Her skin was smooth, her nipples hard, and her legs parted just enough for us to see her pussy. My gaze ran over her red lips and icy ringlets.

Minni had always reminded me of a 1950's movie star. She knew she was gorgeous and used that to her advantage.

"I like tying women up." Her crimson eyes locked on our omega. "I love wrapping them in rope and watching as their breasts fill with blood. They become more tender, their muscles yearning for freedom while aching to stay bonded. I like knife play, collars, leashes, and whips. All sorts of things. Handcuffs, masks. I like to play with my food before I eat it," she said, smirking. "I know they always tell us that's bad manners, but really— the food is mine to do what I please. So why not play with it? Why not make it cry?"

Ember let out a breath, looking from her to me.

I arched a brow, curious about her response. I watched as she pressed her thighs together, her scent becoming heavier with lust.

"I prefer more direct things," I said. "Although what

Minni is talking about can be fun. I have tied her up before and left her for hours."

"Cruel," Minni teased, winking at me. "So mean."

I couldn't help but smile now, either. "You deserved it. But, Ember, just because we both enjoy such things—"

"I've always wanted to try those things," Ember said. "Although rope makes me nervous...."

"Rope isn't for everyone," I said. "However, Minni has suspended me ten feet up in the air before. Any skilled person should be able to tie anyone safely."

"True," Minni said. "Very, very true. Are you going to tell her about the pictures?"

I shot her a dirty look, although I enjoyed the way that Ember's face lit up with interest.

I fought off a groan but still swallowed hard. "I like to take pictures with a camera I have," I said. "It takes black and white Polaroid pictures. I like to keep them. Sexy photos can be a lot of fun."

Ember made a noise. "I...do you want to take pictures of me?"

She had no idea. No fucking idea how much I did.

"Yes," I said. "Now, what do you like?"

"I don't know exactly," she said. "I haven't had the chance to do a whole lot, and so I am new to all of this. But I've had fantasies before. And... I think if I trusted someone, I'd be willing to do a lot."

I glanced up at Minni, another silent agreement.

"We can try whatever you want," Minni said. "I think between the two of us, you'll have fun. And we might as well make this heat memorable. But we need a safe word, and we need to know if you think you have any limits."

Ember nodded, thinking for a moment. "I don't want to be left in the dark. And I don't want to be left alone in general, even if you tie me up. Other than that, I can't think of anything. And for a safe word, 'ducky' works."

"Ducky," we both said, locking that into our minds.

"Excellent," Minni said, tilting her head to the side. "Come here," she said, patting her thigh.

I smiled now, knowing I was going to enjoy this.

Sometimes, I just liked to watch and watching Ember and Minni would be fun.

Ember looked at me. "You can take your pictures if you want."

Fuck.

"I'm going to just watch for now," I said, "but thank you for giving me your consent."

Ember nodded and then slid off the couch onto all fours. I sucked in a sharp breath, watching as she crawled to Minni.

On second thought, perhaps getting the camera wasn't such a bad idea.

CHAPTER SIX

polaroid

MINNI

"I WANT you to say 'My Lady' every time I command you to do something and when you respond to me," I said, slowly spreading my legs further.

Ember had crawled to me and was at the end of the chaise now, her cheeks pink and skin giving off that soft magical glow. Her eyes were wide with lust, her lips parted as she feasted on my body.

I loved the way she looked at me. Like I was her own personal goddess.

I wanted to see that look while I fucked her throat with my strap-on.

Fuck, all the things I wanted to do to her.

The look Lea had given me earlier had been one of warning. One that was a reminder for us to take things slowly with her. But that was easier said than done when she smelled like heaven and was so fucking needy.

"Yes, My Lady," she whispered.

"Oh, you're such a good girl," I purred, spreading my legs further. "Do you want to taste, sweetheart?"

"Please," she whispered.

"Please?" I asked, arching a brow.

"Please, My Lady," she said, correcting herself.

"Good," I said. "And you remember your safeword?"

"Yes, My Lady," she whimpered.

"Good girl," I said.

I slid my hand down to my pussy, running my fingertips over the neatly trimmed triangle. I circled my clit for a moment, my breath hitching.

Even my own body was aching. If I were an omega, I would be in heat, just like my precious little witch.

"Come," I said, placing one of my legs on the back of the chaise.

Ember moved forward, her hands gliding up my calves and thighs. I let out a long hiss, my head tipping back as she buried her face against my pussy. She gave my clit a tentative lick, one that sent a shock wave through me.

Oh fuck.

"Good girl," I hummed, thrusting my hips up against her mouth.

She moaned and began to lick and suck, her fingers testing my entrance as she pleased me.

"Good omega," I said. "Such a good girl pleasing your Lady like this."

I heard the snap of a camera and looked up, pleasure spreading through me as Lea pulled the polaroid picture free.

Fuck, I had missed her. She had unbuttoned the front of her shirt now, her sleeves rolled up as she snapped another picture. I let out a long moan as Ember licked my clit just right, pleasure rolling through me.

It had been too long. Too fucking long. I hadn't been with anyone since Lea and I had split, just relying on my toys to get me off.

It wasn't the same. It wasn't the same as having an eager tongue and a heated gaze.

Ember moaned, her fingers pushing inside of me. She began to move them as she licked, making me groan again.

Lea came closer to us, going around behind me so that she could watch.

I tipped my head back, watching her now. Her green skin caught highlights of gold from the lamps around the room, her tusks gleaming as she smiled.

"Kiss me," I whispered.

Lea looked down, her honey-brown eyes burning with indecision.

"Please," I all but begged.

Lea raised the camera, snapping a photo that I would try to steal away later.

"Bitch," I hissed, narrowing my eyes.

She smirked. "Sorry, it's just that I've always wanted a picture of you begging, and this is the first one I've managed to get."

I scoffed, but it was muffled as she leaned down and kissed me. Everything melted away, and I groaned against her mouth.

Ember pulled her tongue away for a moment, and I broke my kiss with Lea, looking down at her.

I would have time to tie her up this week, to collar and pull her around my home on a leash, to spank her, and do all types of things.

But right now, I wanted to feel her against me.

"Take off your clothes," I said. "Now."

"Yes, My Lady," she breathed.

Her lips glistened with my essence as she stood. I watched as she undressed, letting out a long moan.

Fuck, she was gorgeous. I wanted to sink my teeth into every curve, to taste her everywhere.

"Beautiful," Lea said, her voice soft and husky.

I sat up and grabbed Ember's hand, pulling her onto the chaise. I pushed her down and then straddled her, yanking her head back so that she looked up at me.

She was panting now, her heart pounding in her chest. I could hear her blood rushing.

"My Lady," she gasped.

"Yes," I said, baring my fangs.

She arched her head farther back, offering me her neck. The motion made me pause for a moment, the tenderness of it endearing in a way that I hadn't expected.

I raised my hand, dragging the tip of my nail down the artery that pulsed there. I leaned down, pressing my lips against her sweet skin. I used the tip of my tongue to trace the vein again, that fierce hunger returning with a vengeance.

If I hadn't had centuries of self-control as practice, I would have ripped into her. There would have been a time that I would have drunk from her over and over until I was sated and she was drained.

But I wasn't that vampire anymore.

"Not yet," I whispered. "I want you to cum again first before I taste you, sweetheart."

She nodded, her eyes fluttering.

I kissed up her neck, up her jaw to where I found her lips. She tasted like Lea, tasted like me.

She tasted like her.

I groaned as her lips parted, taking me in. We kissed, the two of us moaning together. I ran my hands down her body, cupping her breasts. She whimpered as I began to circle her nipples.

She was so sensitive, so sweet.

I could feel myself getting more and more wet. I heard the sound of the camera again, snapping another picture that I would steal.

With a little growl, I pushed Ember down harder onto the cushion beneath us. She gasped as I pinned her down and spread her legs. I lowered myself, angling our bodies so that my pussy pressed against hers.

"My Lady," she moaned.

I slowly started to grind against her, sucking in a breath as pleasure unfurled. I began to move against her, meeting her little thrusts with my own.

My pussy pulsed as we found a rhythm, the feeling of her clit against mine driving me crazy. I groaned, my head falling back.

I heard the click of the camera and couldn't help but grin.

Ember gasped, her face twisting in ecstasy as we moved in tandem. I gripped her thighs, enjoying the way my nails dug into her skin.

"I'm so close," she cried. "I'm so close!"

"Good," I rasped.

I leaned back, planting my hands on the cushion as we ground against each other.

Fuck, I was close too.

Ember let out a cry, her muscles tensing as her orgasm crashed into her. Watching her cum was enough to make me cum, pleasure bursting through me.

I cried out as I came, my body trembling. I was left gasping, my cunt dripping against hers.

Lea came up to the two of us now, finally undressed.

"Let me clean you both up," she said.

I could barely form words, so I just nodded, letting out a breathless laugh as she knelt down and moved both of us.

She leaned down between my legs, and I gasped as her tongue found my clit.

"Fuck," I hissed.

She knew she could make me cum again with just that orc tongue of hers. I cried out as her tongue pushed inside of me, her thumb circling my clit. She was quick, the movements fierce and enough to have me screaming.

Another orgasm crashed into me, blinding me as she licked up every drop of my release. She let go with a satisfied chuckle, and I melted against the couch, my muscles relaxing.

Ember let out a little yelp as Lea kissed up her body, parting her legs so that she could clean her up. I watched with a sated gaze as Lea made her cry and moan, the sounds bringing me joy.

Ember's body arched against her, her sharp cry ringing through my home as she came again. Lea stayed there, getting every drop up and lapping at her until she was finished.

She moaned, melting against the chaise too.

"Are you okay?" I asked.

Ember held up a thumbs up symbol, making Lea and me snort.

"Lea," I purred.

Lea looked up, arching a brow.

"I will make it up to you," I said, "when I can think straight."

Lea laughed, her expression one I had missed.

"Oh, you will," Lea said. "Both of you will tomorrow.

But for tonight, I'm fine with being on clean-up. Making both of you cum makes me happy."

Ember raised her head, her eyes glazed over from cumming twice in a row. It wasn't as much as both Lea, and I knew we could make happen, but today had been a long day.

"I want to make you cum, too," she said.

"You will," Lea said, winking.

She stood up and grabbed her camera, along with the photos.

"I want to see them," I said.

"Nope," Lea snickered. "Not until I say so."

"Hey!" I hissed, but she was already leaving the room.

Ember let out a giggle and shifted, moving so that she could lay her head on me. I narrowed my eyes, amused at how I was immediately distracted.

"Fine," I sighed. "I'll chase her down later."

Ember nodded, her arms wrapping around me.

Yep, I was going nowhere.

CHAPTER SEVEN
tuesday

EMBER

I'D WOKEN up this morning and realized that it was Tuesday.

Tuesday.

The amount of convincing it had taken to get Lea and Minni to allow me to come to the office had been hard work. By the time we'd gone through a third set of arguments, I had ended up practically signing my soul away.

Yes, I was in heat. Yes, I just wanted sex. But gods damn it, this was the interview I had been working for. I had to do it.

The three of us rode up the elevator, the silent storm that Minni was radiating making me nervous.

"The moment you need to go, we're going," Lea grumbled. "I can't believe we even agreed."

"I can't miss this interview," I said.

"I could interview you at home and determine the best

way to fuck you senseless," Minni said, studying her sharp nails.

The same nails that had dug into me while she made me see god last night.

I blew out a breath, trying to control the wave of heat.

"This is a dumb idea," Lea sighed. "Have you heard of rescheduling? I already texted Inferna and I know she would be fine with it."

"I have been working for this for a long time," I snapped, looking at Lea. "I know this is stupid. But I want this fucking job. I just want to be normal," I said.

"You're not normal," Minni hissed. "You're an omega witch in heat, and you're not going to last through this stupid interview. There is nothing wrong with being rescheduled, Ember."

"Yes there is!" I barked.

Minni stared at me for a moment, her eyes widening.

I drew in a steadying breath, trying not to cave into my emotions. Into my heat. Tears filled my eyes, but I held them back.

"I need this," I whispered. "I need this for myself. I've been working so hard for this. It's all I can think about since it was announced. I have never been able to do anything for myself like this, and I...I need this. That's all."

Minni and Lea nodded.

"Plus," I said, "we agreed that after, I will take the rest of the week off."

I could feel the two of them exchanging looks.

"You also agreed that you're moving in," Minni said.

I made a face as the elevator doors slid open.

I *had* said that, even though that was insane.

"So we'll pack your stuff this weekend," Minni chimed.

"And at least we were able to get you a to-go bag for the week."

I sighed in defeat as we stepped out into the office. I headed for my desk, not surprised to see that Jaehan was already in his seat. Lea followed me as I went to my chair.

Jaehan looked up, scowling. "What do you think you're doing?"

"I'm here for my interview," I said.

He stared at me for a moment and shook his head, scoffing. "Seriously. After all the hell you've given me. Just reschedule it. Alex, of all people, would understand."

"Don't start," I snapped.

"We tried," Lea growled, taking the desk right next to mine.

RIP to anyone who was using it. It was very much her desk now.

Jaehan shook his head. "Stubborn."

"She is," Lea said.

I gave her a dark look. "We made an agreement."

"Yes, and the agreement didn't say anything about me not giving you shit for this decision," Lea said.

Jaehan snorted, and I gave him a dirty look too.

"You're going to upset all the monsters," Jaehan said.

"I'm controlling it," I said, turning on my computer. "I'm checking my email really quickly and then I will head up to Alex's office."

I ignored both of their looks.

I was in control, I reminded myself.

"Good morning."

The three of us looked up to see Alex. My heart started to pound, all of the nerves about this interview rising up. What if I said something wrong? What if I fucked it up? I had rehearsed this in my mind so many times, but even seeing Alex was enough to make me feel like I was dying.

"Morning," I squeaked.

Alex froze in place like he was looking at a ghost, his blue eyes zeroing in on me. "For fuck's sake. What are you doing at work, Ember?"

"I am here for my interview," I said, looking back at my computer.

"I don't think it's a good idea—"

"It's only an hour," I pleaded, looking back up at him.

Alex shook his head, running gloved fingers through his hair. "Ember, we could have interviewed you online. On a call. We could have rescheduled. I can interview you another time."

I felt my world starting to fall apart. "No. I'm already here," I said, swallowing hard.

"No," Alex said. "Go home. We will talk about this another day."

He started to turn to walk away, but I jumped up from my seat. "I'm already right here!" I shouted.

Everyone stared at me, the office growing silent.

"Okay. Leave. Both of you. I'd like to talk to her alone," Alex said.

"No," Lea said. "I'm supposed to stay with her."

"Ah, yes, I know," Alex quipped. "That was my idea. But you can leave her with me. Go catch up with your other mate."

Lea all but scoffed. "Minni isn't...."

Alex halted her words with one look, his gaze cutting like a scalpel.

"I will be okay," I whispered, looking at her.

I'd just yelled at my boss.

The one who was supposed to interview me.

I bit back tears, wishing I could run now.

Jaehan stood up from his desk and shook his head, leaving us. Lea stood too, lowering her face next to mine for a moment.

"I will kill you if a single hair is out of place on her head," Lea said, looking at Alex. "It'll be a good old-fashioned orc killing too. Intestines strung up everywhere, and your head on a spike."

"Lea!" I hissed, but her words startled me enough that the tears went away again.

"He's your boss, sweetheart, not mine. I'll be over there."

I watched as she left us, crossing the room to the desks that belonged to Jaehan's mates.

Alex cleared his throat and took the desk across from me. He moved the computers out of the way, pushing the monitors to the side.

"I'm sorry I yelled," I said. "I've been wanting to interview with you for this position and I've been working so hard. I have all these things I've done to gain experience, and I know I'm new. I promise I'm not normally one to yell, I just–"

"Ember," Alex said, his voice almost fatherly. "With everything that has happened, this is not a good idea. It concerns me that you're here right now."

Concern?

"Why do you care?" I asked.

I knew why he cared.

It wasn't something either one of us had discussed. It wasn't something either one of us would do either.

When the fear demon attacked our group, I was able to stop it, but only because of Alex. It wasn't something we'd shared with the others. They believed that everyone had

TUESDAY · 61

woken up from nightmares and Alex and Billy had been gone.

Alex knew what he was doing and was a lot stronger than anyone knew, just like I was.

Still, the encounter with the demon hadn't been our first one.

There had been a time when everything started where he had interfered.

He had been the reason Cinder had the chance to give services to Aamon in exchange for my safety.

He'd been fighting this fight as much as he could, but now everything was coming to a head.

Alex knew me in a way the others didn't. Not even my sibling. Alex knew me because of my power and because I was the omega who had been spared from Aamon during all of this.

"You're taking a needless risk," he whispered. "After everything, this is just a risk. I am looking forward to interviewing you. And between us, Ember, you're the only one who has even applied. You have a very good chance at getting the position. But you can't get the job if you're dead, can you? I'm trying to change things before they get worse," Alex said. "Plus, you have Minni and Lea as your mates to keep you distracted. Stay with them, and we'll interview when your heat is finished. The job will wait for you."

"They aren't my mates," I said.

He gave me a flat expression. "Did you hear anything I just said?"

"Of course," I said. "I just... they aren't my mates."

"Yet," he responded.

"They aren't," I said. "I'm a loner. They're just with me to help with this random heat."

"Don't lie to me," Alex said, his expression becoming

closer to a glare. "Why can't you just be happy you've found your mates?"

"I'm not lying," I said, crossing my arms. "And fuck you. Why can't you just make Alfred disappear?"

Alex groaned. "Gods, okay. I was out of line with that. I'm just trying to help you."

"And I'm trying to get this interview over with."

"Well, again. Not happening. Don't come back to work this week after today, or I will personally kick you out. Your life isn't worth your pride. Being in heat isn't a curse, Ember."

It sure as hell felt like it at the moment.

"Why can't you just interview me?"

"Because, I don't want to and I'm the boss. Now, go. I'll see you next week."

Alex left me without another word, leaving me in a ball of emotions. I glared at my computer screen and then dragged the monitor back in place.

More than anything, I had wanted to stay home this morning. I had wanted to just lie in bed and enjoy Minni and Lea. But, this interview had been the one thing that I had been working towards and wanting for so long.

It was stupid, but coming in today had been one part pride and one part wanting to just fucking get the job.

Being in heat isn't a curse.

I looked up, meeting Lea's gaze. She had never looked away during the entire talk with Alex. She arched her brow, waiting for me to ask her to come back.

Last night felt like a dream. All of the things I had done with her and Minni had left me feeling things I had never felt before.

I liked them both way more than I wanted to.

Way, way more.

I tore my gaze away as heat rushed over me, need blooming. I let out a short gasp and stood.

A couple of growls echoed through the office, and I knew I was attracting attention now.

I could also feel Lea already moving towards me.

Tears blurred my vision, and I crossed the office, ignoring everyone as I rushed down the hall. Lea's footsteps echoed behind me as I slipped into an empty conference room.

I turned to slam the door shut, but a set of manicured fingers shoved it open.

Minni stepped inside, followed by Lea, who then slammed the door. The wall thundered as she twisted the lock.

I made a helpless noise, throwing my hands up. I had wasted their time by coming in today. I had wasted everyone's time.

"Ember," Minni said, her voice soft.

My head snapped up, and I looked at her through blurry eyes.

I had expected her to be mad at me. Angry that I hadn't listened to her or Lea. I had expected her to be mad at me, to yell at me, to be disappointed.

But neither of them looked at me like that.

Both of them looked at me with expressions of worry. The same soft expressions they had last night when they were making sure I was okay.

It broke me.

I let out a choked sob, and Lea opened her arms. I rushed to her, burying my face into her clothes.

This wasn't fair. None of this was fair. And why would they look at me like that?

"Ember," Minni said softly.

I felt her hand rest on my lower back.

For a vampire with looks that could kill, she was more comforting than anything else in my life.

Lea let out a sigh, but it was one that felt like a breath of relief, not of disappointment.

Tears rolled down my cheeks, and I felt like everything was caving in. This was all my fault. I had wasted their time and had even put the office in danger by being so reckless.

The thought that I had fucked up felt like a weight shoving me down, holding me under to drown. Another sob shook my shoulders, and I cried. I cried and cried, all while Lea held me and Minni petted me.

"You know," Lea said, pulling away to cup my face. I tried to pull away, but she held me still. "You're an ugly crier, but you're still gorgeous."

That loosened another sob from me, my mind still spinning.

She thumbed away the tears even as they kept coming. She held me that way until they slowly stopped, the panic that had gripped me, releasing me one claw at a time.

"Whatever Alex said to you, I'm going to kill him," Lea said.

"No," I sniffled. "No. This isn't because of him. I just... I mean, he said some things that are right. And... well. I'm here because of him. And I should try to keep everyone safe."

"That's not your job," Minni said. "You don't get paid for that, honey. The two of us do." She stepped up behind me, her arms winding around my waist. "It's going to be okay."

"It doesn't feel like it will be," I whispered. "It doesn't feel like that. I hate being an omega. My entire life, I've had to deal with this, and it's done nothing but hurt those around me. The only reason Cinder and I were able to live differently was because Alex interfered. And I don't think Cinder knows that. No one knows that. But I know that because the day I was let out of their dark confines was when I met him. This has been something that has been going on for a long time, and the fact that more and more people keep getting hurt.... I can't help but feel like it's my fault."

"Ember," Lea said firmly. "I know you feel that way, but none of this has been your fault. You haven't done anything wrong. You were a victim in all of this, just like Calen and Jaehan and some of the other omegas. Even Cinder too. All of this has been because there is an evil motherfucker out there who wants to use all of your magic, and that's not fair. He's the reason all of this has happened. The fact that you have heats— even if he wasn't lurking around, you would still need to stay home and take care of yourself. It would be no different from calling in sick. And no matter where or who you work for, taking sick time shouldn't be like this, even for a big interview. Life happens. You have no obligation to come in. This office can run without you, and that job will still be waiting when you get back."

"Not to mention, you don't get paid nearly enough to feel like you should sacrifice your health for them," Minni said. "And this is a health issue."

I let out a long breath and leaned forward, planting my forehead on Lea's chest. I let their words sink in, trying to sort through all the jumbled thoughts. Trying not to feel like a failure.

"I want to go home," I whispered.

"Okay," Minni said. "We'll take you home."

CHAPTER EIGHT

worry

LEA

I SAT in an office with Inferna, Art, Alex, and Cinder. My leg was drumming up and down as I spoke. I was ready to get in my car and drive home, but I needed to talk to all of them first.

"I think we'll stay with her the rest of the week," I said to them.

Minni had already driven Ember back to her house, but I had decided to stay behind, so I could meet with the four of them. My car was still in the garage from the other day anyway, so getting to Minni's wouldn't be an issue.

"I'm worried," Inferna sighed, taking a seat in her chair.

The four of us were in her office, the world outside full of snow and ice. There was a storm forecasted for tonight, which also made me nervous.

Minni was a vampire, therefore she didn't need to think about warm food and water and all of the things that were now on my mind. If the power went out, we would need to be prepared, although that was unlikely to happen.

"Everyone is going home early today," Alex said, glancing outside. "I don't like how the weather is shaping up. And while the human infrastructure is sound enough, I don't trust anything."

"Me either," I said.

Art and Cinder both nodded, the two of them stewing in their thoughts. Inferna looked up at her partner, her lips tugging into a soft smile.

They were too fucking cute all of the time. All of the looks they exchanged in passing at work, the moments they would steal Calen away. Calen was adorable too.

I was happy for my friend. More than happy. She had found love with two people, and they both worshiped her.

"I want her to be safe," Cinder sighed. "I'm worried about her and would feel better if she were with Mich, Lora, and me."

"She's with an ancient vampire and an orc," I said. "She will be safe, Cinder. I can promise you that."

Cinder held my gaze for a moment. Stubbornness must run in their blood because Cinder wore the same expression I'd seen on Ember earlier.

I wondered about the rest of their family. What had happened to their parents? Did they have anyone, or had it really just been the two of them?

The thought made me sad. My family could be annoying at times, but if I ever needed something, I could call. I could show up at my parents' cabin tomorrow, and they would welcome me with open arms, without question, and with nothing but love. And food. Lots and lots of food.

They'd want to meet Ember. And they would be happy to hear that Minni and I might be back together.

"I won't let her come back to the office this week," I said. "I don't know what that demon is up to, and I don't want it coming our way. I think staying out of the way is the best thing she can do."

Alex nodded. "She's very stubborn, but I'm glad she agreed to go."

"Well, whatever you said to her didn't exactly leave her feeling warm and fuzzy," I said, giving him a hard look.

Cinder, Art, and Inferna all looked at him, their eyes sharp.

Alex shrugged. "She needed a push. Being here while in heat is dangerous, even without all of the events that have happened. The wrong monster gets a whiff of her and—"

"They end up dead," I growled, glaring. "And I think that's the wrong way to look at it. Monsters can control themselves. An omega shouldn't be the one to bear that responsibility. She needs to stay home because while in heat, she's running a fever and needs care. And sex. Not because monsters catch her scent and get horny."

"Agreed," Cinder said, wincing. "Although, let's please not talk about my sister needing sex."

I snorted and grinned. "Fine. Alright, I am going. I need to drive home, and I'd like to stop and get groceries so that we can eat well. We all have our phones, so if you need something, just call. Inferna, can I talk to you alone for a moment?"

Inferna nodded, standing from her chair. "I'll go down to your car with you."

I smiled, and the two of us left the other three, heading down the hall to the elevator. We stepped inside, and as soon as the doors shut, I let out a sigh.

Inferna put her hand on my shoulder, offering me comfort. "Are you okay?"

"I am," I said. "Just worried. This is a mess, Inferna. And it's dangerous. I'm just concerned that something is going to happen."

Inferna nodded and pulled me into a hug. "It'll be okay. So far, all of us have made it out okay. We're going to beat him."

She sounded so sure, which gave me comfort. But then again, Inferna had always been so sure of the things she wanted, even if they were impossible for everyone else around her to do.

We'd been friends since I was adopted. Our parents had gone way back, back to when they were all discovering love. Back when some of the witches and vampires had been a problem.

Now we were adults with problems like they had dealt with, living in a world where monsters were becoming more accepted— but all of the old problems were still the same.

There were demons like Alfred, AKA Aamon, who liked to use their abilities to take advantage of humans and creatures. There were monsters who still despised humans, and even other monsters too. They wanted to hurt them, to hunt them.

Then there were creatures like us. Ones who liked to live a normal life and just wanted to exist in peace.

Inferna sighed and pulled back as the doors slid open to the parking garage. The brisk air hit me, and I shivered as we stepped out.

"How are you and Minni?" Inferna asked.

I made a face, one that said a lot more than I would have liked, but I had never done well at hiding my feelings. "We're...healing. I don't know what will happen there. Both of us are her mates."

Inferna nodded, her dark eyes softening. "I am happy

for all three of you but a little worried too. Ember has been through a lot and aside from the love Cinder has for her, she doesn't know what it's like to be cared for. And you and Minni...well, you know my opinions. I never thought the two of you should have broken up. You loved each other."

"I still love her," I said. "But I think we both needed some time. It's hard, you know. She's been around a lot longer than either one of us have. In fact, I think she's not too much younger than your Dad."

"Oh, she's not that old," Inferna snorted. "But that's never really been an issue for our kind, right? Age is but a number at a certain point. My parents seem to be just fine."

I grinned, thinking about Peter. That guy was a champ, although supposedly Dante had relaxed significantly since they'd had Inferna and her brother Acheron. Or Archie, as a few of us called him.

"Have you talked to your brother?" I asked.

Inferna made a face now as we walked to my car. "Nope. He's out doing whatever he does. I emailed him a while back. He talks to my Dad a lot, but he and Papa don't speak much still."

I felt a little prick of sadness. "I guess as long as you're still trying."

"I can't blame him," Inferna sighed. "He has it rough."

"It's been a few years, though," I said. "But... I know how family can be. Simon and I still fight at every holiday."

Simon was one of my brothers and a complete asshole most of the time. He meant well, but I was looking forward to the day he met someone that put him on his ass.

Inferna shrugged. "Family is great, but it's not perfect, and even though I have been fortunate, I will not force someone into my life who doesn't have any interest. Blood or not. I'm here for him, but I can't stress about it. I miss him but hell, I don't even think I've talked to Calen or Art about him yet. They saw the family photos that Papa has hung up in the living room, but they didn't ask."

"Well," I said, stopping at my car finally. "The three of you are still very new. And isn't that the fun thing about being with someone? You get to know them over time. You find out new things about them and discover more about the things that hurt them. The longer you're with someone, the more you love them as you find out more about the little things. Like their favorite soap from when they were a kid, or why they hate shrimp."

Inferna grinned, her tail swishing behind her. "True. Lea, keep me updated, please. And if you need anything, call us immediately. A little ice and snow never stopped us, and Art can portal us straight to you."

"Thanks," I said.

"Oh, and Lea. Not that I told you this but... Ember already is chosen for that job. So, maybe let it slip that she'll get it."

I hesitated for a moment. "I think she wants to feel like she earned it."

"She has. Which is why the interview is just a formality."

I smiled. "Alright, when you put it that way. Time to go face the masses grocery shopping, and then check on Minni and Ember."

CHAPTER NINE

ropes

MINNI

EMBER RAN her fingertips over the purple rope, her eyes wide and scent making me want to shove her down and fuck her again.

She was needy again, her heat making her insatiable. The only thing I could think of doing now was tying her up and making her cum over and over until Lea got home.

By the time Lea got home, I would have Ember tied up and begging.

"Do you want to try it out?" I asked. "We could start with some simple ties."

"Yes," Ember said, giving me an eager look. "I want to try."

"Okay," I said, grinning. "I will get everything then. Go wait in my room."

I could hear her heart beating a little faster, her blood rushing in her veins as she gave me a quick kiss and then rushed off to my room.

I smiled to myself as I gathered up the ropes and safety shears. I knew exactly how I would tie her up, depending on if she enjoyed it or not. We'd start with a chest harness, and then if she felt good about it, I would tie her hands and feet.

I left the room where I kept all of my fun things, a small office space dedicated to all sorts of things, from paddles to ropes to a bench that was perfect for bending someone over and pegging them.

We would come back to this room, but for the moment, tying her up on my bed would be perfect.

I went down the hall to my room and stepped into the doorway, biting my lip. Ember was on my bed, naked with her legs spread. Her pussy glistened in the lighting, and her eyes heated.

"You're such a pretty girl," I hummed.

I ran the tip of my tongue over my fangs and crept closer, stopping at the foot of my bed. It was a king-sized four-poster bed with canopy drapes and a mirror above the headboard.

Oh yes, I designed this bed with many things in mind.

"Please," Ember whispered. "I need you."

"I know you do, sweetheart," I purred, setting my rope down. "Come here."

She sat up and crawled to the end of the bed. I cupped her face, drawing her into a heated kiss. She melted beneath my touch, the taste of her making me groan.

"Okay," I said, breaking this kiss. "Let's get you all tied up."

I had Ember stand up in front of me, making her lift her arms as I started with a chest harness. Her little noises were enough to have my own pussy pulsing with need, my hunger for her blood growing with every moment. She let out a soft hiss as the rope dragged over her skin and then a whimper as my fingers ran across her.

"How does it feel?" I asked, wrapping the rope around her ribs and then crossing it over her breasts.

"Good," she whispered. "I like how it feels. I want you to keep going."

"Okay," I said. "If you want me to stop, just make sure to tell me."

"Yes, My Lady," she said.

I paused for a moment, a soft growl of pleasure leaving me. My little omega knew exactly what to say to me.

I gripped her hair and pulled her head back, planting another kiss on her soft lips before going back to tying.

After a few moments, the chest harness was tied. Her breasts were beautifully framed by the vibrant purple, her blood still singing in her veins.

I pushed her back onto the bed, making her squeal as I placed her in the center. I grabbed one of her wrists and started to tie, making the knots thick so that they would be safe to pull against. I did the same to her other hand and then bound them together, pinning them above her head.

I tied it to the headboard and sat back, looking down at her. Her eyes were wide, her chest lifting and falling with breaths.

I smiled and leaned down, tracing the tip of one of my nails over the rope, over her breast, to her nipple that was waiting to be licked and bitten. She gasped as I pricked it, her hips bucking up.

"Oh," I said. "I like watching you squirm."

I moved down on the bed and grabbed her ankle, taking my time to bind her and bring the rope to the corner post of the bed. I tied it quickly, enjoying the way her eyes widened as she realized she was about to be trapped.

Trapped and mine completely.

I growled as I did the same to the other ankle, tying until her legs were now completely spread, her body trapped to my will.

"How do you feel, princess?" I asked, crawling up the bed to her side.

"Good," she gasped. "I like how the rope feels. I like knowing that I'm yours. But please...please touch me."

I smiled and rolled off the bed again, going to a mirrored dresser that sat on the opposite side of the room. I opened up the top drawer and pulled out a vibrator.

I was going to make her scream.

I went back to the bed and climbed over her, straddling her stomach. She sucked in a breath with a moan as I leaned down, my face hovering over hers.

"Please," she whispered. "I'm begging you."

"This isn't begging, sweetheart," I said. "This is you just telling me what you want. If you're going to beg, then actually beg."

"Please!" She said, her voice a little louder.

"No," I said, snickering. "No. Learn how to beg properly, and then I might consider it."

"My Lady," she gasped, trying to writhe beneath me. "I need you. I need you to play with me. I need to cum so bad. I'm dying."

"Mmm, dying, huh? I see," I said.

"I will die if you don't make me cum," she whispered.

"You're a little dramatic, honey," I said, but I still slid down her body to where her legs were spread. "You really want me to touch you?"

"Yes," she said eagerly. "Please. Please!"

She was going to regret that.

But I still smiled, flashing my fangs as I lowered my lips

to her pussy. I flicked my tongue out, running it over her clit.

Her entire body reacted, yanking against the ropes. I grinned as she writhed, enjoying her little noises.

I wondered for a moment if she'd ever even used a vibrator. I licked her again, tasting her before pulling back again.

Her head lifted, and she shot me a glare.

I held up the vibrator. "Look at me like that again, and I'll torture you with this and stop once you're about to cum."

Her head fell back again, and I smirked, hitting the on button.

"Such a brat," I teased. "Just because you're in heat doesn't mean you get endless orgasms."

"My Lady," she moaned.

"Have you ever used one of these?" I asked over the low vibrating noise.

"No," she said.

"Even better," I chuckled, lowering the head to her clit.

The sound that left her the moment it touched her made me incredibly happy. Her voice echoed through the room as she cried out, the ropes holding her in place as I held the toy to her dripping cunt.

She let out a scream, her head tossing back into the pillows with a cry. She let out a stream of curses as I angled the vibrator perfectly on her clit, and then began to tease her entrance with two of my fingers.

"Oh god," she cried. "Oh my god."

I smirked, slowly easing my fingers inside of her. She was trying so desperately to pull away but couldn't. She was my trapped little pet, tied up and aching to cum.

"So wet," I said. "Just dripping for me like a good little slut."

She gasped as I bit my bottom lip, my fangs piercing my

own skin as I watched her face. There wasn't much else that was more perfect than watching a woman's expression when she was about to cum.

Her words weren't coherent as she writhed against the rope, her body quivering.

I pulled the vibrator back.

Okay. There was something more perfect than that expression. The one that a woman gives when she's denied being able to cum.

"You bitch," she hissed.

I grinned now, licking up the drops of my blood from my mouth. "I told you, sweetheart. And also, here you are again. Being a silly little brat."

"Let me cum," she rasped.

"No," I said, arching a brow. "Why would I let you when you're being so rude? Why would I give you the pleasure of that?"

"Because you love me," she said, pleading with her eyes like a little puppy.

I narrowed my gaze. "Love is a strong word, princess."

Ember pulled against the ropes again, letting out a frustrated noise. "Yes, well, I don't make the rules."

I couldn't help but laugh now. My sweet Ember was not only stubborn, she thought she would be able to get what she wanted by just telling me.

"Cute," I said, lowering myself between her legs. "Very cute. Well, perhaps I do love you already. Perhaps I want to make you my mate forever. But neither of those things means I'm going to let you cum right now. But you know what I will do? I'll take a taste. Stay still, little pet. I wouldn't want to hurt you."

Before she could give me a sour comeback, I sank my teeth into the softest part of her inner thigh. Her cry echoed out, but it was drowned out by the euphoria I got from tasting her blood. I groaned, sinking my teeth in further as I tasted her.

The heat of her blood filled my mouth, the taste of her omega heat and magic making me feel high. I swallowed it down, enjoying the way it sated my hunger.

I groaned and released her, licking my lips as red dripped from the bite mark.

I realized that she was panting and moaning, but not from pain.

From pleasure.

I leaned in again, higher up on her thigh this time. I started to rub her clit with my fingers in slow circles as I pressed my fangs to her skin, sinking them in.

Fuck, her scream was perfect. Edged with pleasure, sharp enough to cut diamonds. She filled my mouth as I kept circling her clit. Her hips thrust up, her body becoming more and more desperate.

Finally, I heard the first real beg.

"Please don't stop," she rasped. "Please, My Lady. Please!"

I grinned as I drank her blood, increasing the pressure of my fingers. Her body arched up, her lungs releasing another sharp cry.

I would give in to her request, but only because I knew how much it took for her to truly beg me.

"Please!" she sobbed. "Please don't stop! Ah!"

I sank my fangs in further, not even minding the fact that I was starting to get dangerously close to giving in to my desire to fully mate her. Every second that passed that I drank more of her became stronger. I was sure she had to be mine forever.

I started to rub her clit faster, sending her straight to the edge.

She cried out as she came, her entire body tensing under the release. I could feel all of the endorphins hit. I tasted them in her blood. I groaned, feeding off them as she came.

I withdrew my fangs and leaned back, watching as her breasts heaved and her eyes fluttered.

"Be my mate," I whispered. "Please."

"Yes," she whimpered.

I didn't hesitate. Didn't think. I didn't give either of us a moment to second guess things. Instead, I held my wrist to my fangs and tore into it before straddling her again, offering her the black blood that dripped from me.

Her eyes flew open, holding on to mine as her lips parted and she started to suck.

I gasped as I felt...warmth? Life? Pain? Pleasure?

So many things moved through me, spreading through my body like wildfire as she drank more. I pulled my wrist away, only to hear a spell slip from her lips.

Mate. She was mine. I knew she was mine from the moment I had seen her, and now....

Now, she was truly mine.

I felt the spell take root, the bonds wrapping us in invisible threads. She gasped, the sound of her heart hammering through me as if my own were still beating.

I leaned down and kissed her, feeling tears slip from my eyes.

I pulled back, immediately undoing the ropes. It didn't take too long as I moved quickly, freeing her from the binds. I threw it to the floor, climbed onto the bed, and pulled her into a hug.

She turned over, pressing her face against my breasts. She breathed in my scent, and I could feel...*her*. Her feelings, her thoughts, her worries. I could feel the tornado of emotions that swirled inside of her, so many that I lost count.

I held her close, my eyes widening as I started to realize what we had just done.

"Hey, you two, I'm home!" Lea's voice called from downstairs.

"Shit," Ember whispered.

Fuck.

I had told Lea we would take things slowly. This was the *exact* opposite of that.

"It's okay," I said, trying to soothe her worries. "It's okay, Ember. Just rest, love. I'll go talk to her."

Ember started to argue, but I found myself holding my hand to her head and using my ability to make her sleep.

Her words fell silent, her breaths softening.

I sat up just as Lea came to the doorway. She froze, her eyes widening.

"You didn't."

"Lea," I said. "Let me explain—"

"We said that we would take things slowly," Lea said, the pain in her voice a knife through my chest.

"Lea," I whispered, climbing out of bed. "Let me—"

She shook her head, glaring at me. "All I've ever done is give to you. I gave you all of me. I changed my life for you, changed the way I lived for you. I gave you everything that I could possibly give. And you've never given me one damn thing. Not even this," she said, her voice low and cool. "You agreed we would take it slow with her, and I come home out of a fucking snowstorm from the grocery store to you *mating* her!"

I crossed my room to her, reaching for her. Lea slapped my hand away, her glare making me panic.

"Lea, please," I said. "It just happened. I didn't plan this. I didn't plan for any of this."

"You always said you'd never take a full mate," she said.

Another set of words that felt like a knife wound.

"Lea," I whispered. "I still love you."

She shook her head, heading out of the room. "Leave me alone. I'm going to make dinner, and I want some time alone. Even from her, if she wakes from the sleep you just put her in."

Before I could say anything else, she went down the stairs, leaving me alone with my new mate.

CHAPTER TEN

waffle wednesday

EMBER

I SAT STRAIGHT UP in bed, my heart pounding.

The sound of water running in the bathroom that joined this bedroom helped soothe me, but I still felt a flicker of worry.

I *felt* Minni.

She was my mate. I had told her to make me her mate. I had even spoken the mating spell that would bind us together forever.

I stared at the wall, my thoughts registering.

I expected to be filled with regret, but the only thing I could think of right now was Lea.

I slid out of bed, grabbing a robe that was tossed over a velvet chair. I pulled it on, glancing towards the bathroom where Minni was. I lingered for a moment, torn between going to her and checking on Lea.

Minni and I were fine, but I wasn't sure if Lea was okay.

I slipped out of the room, heading downstairs.

Lea was in the kitchen cutting up vegetables. She wore an apron with a tank top underneath, one that let me see her back muscles move as she cooked. Her long hair was swept up into a messy bun, her shoulders tense.

I came through the doorway, freezing as she paused.

She didn't look up at me.

"Lea," I said. "Uh...how's it going?"

"Fine," she said. "I'd like some time alone, Ember."

I was silent for a moment, trying to keep the tears that sprang to my eyes at bay.

"Can we talk first?" I asked, my gut twisting.

"No," she said. "I need time first. I have a temper, and right now, I'm trying my very best to keep it under control. I need time. Breakfast will be ready later. I'm sure you're hungry after being mated and then resting all night."

Fuck. I'd slept through the entire night?

Her words were emotionless, which made me feel even worse. My throat burned, but I nodded, backing out of the kitchen. "Okay," I whispered. "I'll be in the living room."

She didn't respond, her silence answer enough.

I heard a sigh as I left. I went to the chaise that stretched out, grabbed a blanket, and curled up. There was a fireplace on the wall to my right, and at some point, Lea must have started a fire.

I didn't regret what Minni and I had done, but I still felt upset that we had hurt Lea. I didn't know everything about their relationship, but I knew it had to be hard that both of them were mine.

I swallowed hard, thinking about that for a few moments.

Both of them were *mine*. I had two monstrous mates,

and even though I had been so certain that it wouldn't work out, I still wanted to try.

Lea could take all the time she wanted, but I would show her that I could love her just as much. That if we formed a bond, it would be just as sacred.

I looked around the room, realizing that Lea really had been right. I had slept straight through the night. Morning light came through the windows, but it was dulled by the gray skies and snow that was now coming down in sheets.

I sat alone for a few minutes, thinking about everything. I was surprised when I heard movement. I looked up as Lea came into the living room holding two mugs, both of them steaming. I swallowed back tears again as she handed me one of them.

"Coffee," she said, taking a seat in the chair across from me.

"Thank you," I whispered, holding it to my chest. I took a sip, the warmth making me sigh.

She leaned back in the chair, crossing one of her legs over the other. I realized that I could stare at her for hours, studying her muscles and tusks and how pretty she was.

"I'm not mad at you," Lea said, looking up at me. "I want you to know that."

"I don't want you to be mad at Minni either—"

"Darling, Minni has been around for a very long time, and she knew what was happening. Even still, my frustration with her isn't your problem."

"I just..." I trailed off for a moment, trying to find the right words. "I asked her to. I wanted her to. And I don't regret it. I want her just as much as I want you. And I'm coming to terms with the fact that I do have mates. I never thought this would be something that would happen to me."

"Which is why we wanted to take this slowly," Lea said, giving me a gentle smile.

"You're not going to scare me off if you think that's the issue."

"No, I don't think that's it. I think this week could end up getting hellish and that changing all of our lives in the middle of it sounds scary."

She wasn't wrong. It wasn't the weekend yet, and I was still in heat. It was barely Wednesday morning, and I had already taken Minni as a mate. I had even agreed to stay here this week, knowing what that could mean for all three of us.

I had gone to work, too, despite knowing what could have happened.

Sometimes I was too stubborn for my own good. So stubborn that it was difficult to stop myself from doing something, even if I knew it would be better not to.

Even now, I still couldn't find a shred of regret for what had already happened in the last couple of days.

"But, at the end of the day, all three of us are adults," Lea sighed. "And I would be lying if I didn't admit that I was jealous. I want to be your mate, Ember. I want to share my life with you. And these are all things I know right now. I can feel it in my bones that you belong with me, and I've known since the moment I saw you."

Tears blurred my vision, her words burrowing deep into me. How long had I craved to hear such a thing? To hear that someone wanted me for me. That someone wanted to build a life together, and not just because I was an omega witch.

"It's so sudden," Lea said with a shrug. "But love moves at its own pace. It doesn't matter to me if it happens overnight. I feel different. And I know Minni feels the same way. But what *does* matter to me is whether or not we make it through the week without any more pain. The office has already been through a lot. You have been through too much. I am worried that Alfred is lurking, waiting to make a move. Waiting to steal you from me after I've found you."

"Me too," I whispered.

I was worried too. What if Alfred suddenly showed up? I highly doubted that he stuck to a 9 to 5 schedule to create pain and chaos.

"Lea," I said, setting my coffee on the table to my right.

I slid off the chaise, my knees hitting the floor. I then crawled to her, stopping only when I could rest my head on her knees.

Lea sat her coffee to the side, her warm hand settling on the top of my head. She was comforting in a way I had never felt before. A way I had lived without my entire life, but now that I felt it— I never wanted to let it go.

"You're not alone," she said softly. "You will never be alone. You don't have to fight these demons alone anymore. Just like Cinder doesn't have to, either. They have their mates, and now you have yours."

Tears streamed down my cheeks, and I nodded, taking a deep breath and releasing it.

"I don't think I'm good enough," I whispered. "I'm not good enough to have others surround me. To be there for me."

The hand that had been comforting me suddenly smacked the top of my head lightly, startling me. I looked up at her, eyes wide.

"You silly witch," Lea said, cupping my face. "Don't say such things, honey. You are good enough. You deserve to be loved and cared for. You deserve to be cherished. You deserve to be wanted and protected. You deserve to be able to let go of the nightmare that has been following you for years, to finally let go of the darkness that has been clinging to you. And you don't just deserve that from others. You deserve that from yourself too."

I felt my heart break, a crack in the walls I had so carefully crafted. Loving myself, accepting myself. I had been able to do those things on the surface, but deep down, I had always felt like I was cursed. Like I had done nothing but cause others pain.

But now I had someone holding me who told me otherwise. A woman who looked at me like I was the center of her world.

"Love yourself first, Ember," she said. "Then love Minni. Then love me."

"Okay," I whispered. "I will do my best."

"Good," Lea said, her tone finally becoming lighter. "Now. Go get Minni and bring her down for breakfast. She may be a vampire, but she can still enjoy some waffles with us. I'll even give her some blood to drizzle over them."

CHAPTER ELEVEN

unleashed

LEA

BREAKFAST WITH MINNI wasn't as terrible as I had expected it to be, although the look in her eyes bothered me the entire time. I had hurt her.

I had done it on purpose too.

I stole another glance at her, searching for anger. Searching for something that wasn't just a little bit of sadness and a lot of avoidance.

Her blonde hair was still damp from her bath, and for once, she had taken off all her makeup. She was just as beautiful barefaced.

Ember leaned back in her seat with a groan. "I'm full. Those were amazing."

"Thank you, darling," I said, winking at her.

Ember blushed and smiled, taking a sip of her coffee.

"Lea is a good cook," Minni said. "Always has been. Well, at least when it comes to breakfast items."

"True," I chuckled. "My Daddy said it was the way of

the Orc to be able to cook breakfast well. The other meals? Not so much."

Ember giggled. "Your parents sound great."

"They are," I agreed.

"What about you, Minni? Do you have any family?"

Minni laughed, the first real one I had heard in at least 24 hours. "Oh. I guess I haven't told you about them. I do have a family, a coven. About twenty bloodsuckers who are a bit of trouble but mean well."

"They're good," I said, thinking about them. "One of the good vampire families."

"Yes," Minni said, smiling. "Hmm. I guess we will need to find a time to visit them. Perhaps for the holidays."

I raised a brow but didn't disagree.

"We could split between your family and mine. And, of course, seeing Cinder too," Minni said.

"Oh," Ember said, smiling softly. She propped her chin up in her hands, humming. "I think Cinder would like for us to spend New Years together, but the other holidays are up in the air. It feels weird that the end of the year is almost here."

"It does," I said.

This year was ending in a way I could have never expected, either.

"Let's worry about the week ahead of us first," I said. "And then holiday plans. Maybe by then, Alfred will be dead."

"Or at least banished back to hell," Minni said, pressing her lips together. "Maybe Lucifer can pull some strings."

I smirked, shrugging. There was no telling with him. He was a friend of my parents and, from what I had heard, was still a brat sometimes.

"I think Inferna is trying to keep everything from them as much as possible," I said.

Minni sighed. "Yeah. Well, we can handle it. Alfred will get sent back to hell, one way or another."

Ember nodded, her expression becoming almost wistful. "I've never wished someone would disappear, but I wish he would. He's evil and not in a redeemable way."

It was true, from what I had heard anyway. I had yet to lay eyes on the demon, but Inferna and company had been clear.

Alfred, AKA Aamon, was an evil bastard who would chain up every omega and feed off their power forever if he could.

"So," Ember said. "We're here for today. And will be snowed in soon, it seems..."

Her scent hit me, the heat returning with a vengeance. I fought off a low growl, aching to touch her. To pin her against a wall and ravage her.

Fuck, there were too many things that I wanted to do to her.

Minni raised a brow, glancing up at the windows. "Guess that means we will have to keep you warm."

Ember swallowed hard, her eyes widening.

"How about you keep her warm while I clean up?" Minni asked, looking at me.

I stared at her for a moment and then nodded, sliding out of my chair. Ember made a little noise as I went to her, scooping her up and throwing her over my shoulder.

"Hey!" she squealed.

I grinned as I carried her into the living room and then to the staircase.

"You can fight me if you want," I teased, swatting her ass.

I had expected a yelp, but what I got was a moan.

Fucking hell.

Fuck it. It was my turn to make her scream.

I took her back into Minni's room and tossed her onto the bed. This time she did yelp, her words tumbling out as I closed the door behind me.

"Ah, I can't believe you just carried me up the stairs like a cavewoman—"

"Stay," I commanded, leaving the room again.

I went down the hall to the room of all things fun. I had ideas now and knew exactly what I wanted to do.

I took my time as I opened up the drawers, roaming around to find the items I wanted to play with. Minni hadn't changed anything about this place, and I still had some of my clothes here.

I arched a brow and pulled off my tank and sweat pants, trading them for a black sheer bodycon dress. It was short, hugging the tops of my thighs.

I liked wearing suits and vests, but at times like this, I enjoyed the shock and awe of a massive strong orc woman wearing clothing you wouldn't even be able to get away with at a club.

I went back to the closet and pulled out the last item I wanted for the night, smirking at it.

My strap-on.

Damn, I'd really left this behind with her when we had broken up.

Well, I was using this tonight.

It took a couple of minutes to get everything strapped in place and cleaned properly. Along with picking the size of cock I wanted to wield. I ran my hand down the rubber shaft, smiling.

A low whistle came from the door, and I turned, smiling at Minni.

"Fucking hot," Minni said, arching a pale eyebrow. "Fuck. Can I watch?"

"Sure," I said. "Why not? But no interfering unless I tell you you can."

"Okay," she said, giving me a fanged grin. "Gods, don't kill the girl. Save some love for me."

I snorted as I opened up a drawer, picking out a collar and a leash. I also grabbed a ruler for the hell of it.

We weren't at the office today, but... we could still use office equipment for fun.

Minni always had all of the fun items hidden away.

I turned around and went past Minni, back to her bedroom. She followed me inside but immediately slipped to the other side of the room where she could watch quietly.

Ember gasped, her eyes wide. "Oh," she whispered. "Fuck. Lea, you're fucking gorgeous."

She was too damn cute. Her purple hair was ruffled, her skin still giving off the golden sheen of her heat. I could hear her heart pounding, her lips parting with a gasp as she saw what I held in my hands.

And then, she saw what I was wielding.

"Fuck," she whispered.

I went to a chair at the foot of the bed and took a seat, arching a brow.

"Come here, Ember."

She stared at me for a moment and then slid out of bed, slowly walking to me. She stopped when she stood in front of me, her eyes still wide with lust.

"Kneel in front of me," I said, relaxing in my seat.

I parted my legs ever so slightly, and Ember moaned,

her eyes falling to my bare pussy. Her legs buckled, and she knelt, her cheeks now bright pink.

I smiled easily and leaned forward, putting the collar around her neck. She took soft breaths as my fingers brushed over her skin. I looped my finger around the pink leather, tugging her forward.

"Are you going to be a good girl for me?" I whispered, my voice gentle. Gentle yet commanding. Soft but unyielding.

"Yes," she said, her breath hitching.

I lifted the leash and latched the end to the metal loop, winding it around my fist. I tugged, yanking Ember's face closer to mine.

"Yes," she groaned. "Fuck."

"A good little witch," I said, holding her gaze. "For me and me alone. You'll do what I say?"

"Anything," she whispered. "Anything you want."

"Good girl," I praised, leaning back in my chair again.

I studied her for a moment. She was still wearing her robe, but the tie around her waist was starting to come loose.

"Take it off," I said, nodding towards the robe.

Her hands fell to the belt, and she tugged it free, shrugging the robe to the floor. I was presented with her— completely naked and mine. I loved everything about her, from how soft and biteable her breasts looked, to her rounded thighs and stomach, to the freckles here and there that I wanted to lick.

I'd let Minni have her fun, and now it was my turn to devour. To take and make her mine.

I suddenly yanked the leash, enjoying her little yelp as I pushed her face down between my thighs. Even with the strap-on, my pussy was still bare and perfect for her to be able to taste.

She groaned as she realized what I was having her do and didn't hesitate for one moment.

My head fell back as her tongue flicked over my clit, her face buried between my legs. She moaned, licking me like it was the last thing she'd ever do.

I gripped her hair, still keeping the leash taut as she devoured me. My nipples hardened, every little lick sending electric shocks through my body.

"Such an eager tongue," I growled. "A thirsty little witch."

She moaned, her tongue dipping inside of me. I groaned and then pulled her leash back, pulling her lips away. I dragged her into an open-mouth kiss, enjoying the taste of me on her lips.

"Lea," she rasped. "Fuck. I need you."

"Not yet," I said, pulling her over my lap.

She gasped as she realized how I was positioning her, placing her so that her ass was over my knees. My cock smacked against her side, rubbing against her skin.

I ran my palm over her cheeks, squeezing both of them. I spread them, smirking.

"So wet already," I chuckled. "Your pussy is practically begging for me, a little witch in heat."

"Yes," she cried. "Please!"

"No," I said, running my hand over her ass again.

I started to pinch and squeeze, enjoying the way she writhed and moaned and yelped depending on the pain or pleasure I gave her.

"Please," she gasped again.

"Please this, please that," I teased.

I ran my fingers down her ass, all the way down to her

pussy. I dipped them inside of her, feeling how wet she was for me.

I took a deep breath— trying to control myself, trying to control this feeling of absolute need. She was driving me insane, even though I was the one that was in control.

Her scent had me in a vice grip, her heat begging me to do more than just play with her.

But I was more patient than that, and I knew exactly what I wanted to do to her, what I had wanted to do to her since I first saw her.

I picked up the cold ruler from the side table, running the flat side over her skin. She shuddered beneath me, goosebumps rising up over her flesh.

"Do you know what this is?" I asked.

"A ruler," she whispered. "I saw it on the table."

"Yes, it is, my sweet girl," I said. "It's your punishment, your punishment for being a little witch in heat."

I continued to tease her with the flat side of the ruler, pressing it against her body. I traced lines down her ass, down her thighs.

I brought it back up abruptly, giving her a little smack. A little taste of the things I was about to do to her.

Ember let out another breath, shivering as I smiled.

I loved seeing her like this. Needy and aching to be touched.

I had done so many things with so many people over the last few years. But *this*? This felt new. Having her bent over my knees— taking everything I gave her was more than perfect.

She whimpered as she squirmed against me. I tightened my grip, pulling back the ruler before bringing it back down.

The sound of the ruler against her skin echoed

throughout the room, followed by her sharp cry. I groaned, smacking her once more.

Fuck, I was already wet too.

The ruler left a nice mark on her skin, red blooming across her golden flesh.

"Remember your safe word," I said.

She nodded, her lips parting on a soft breath. I paused for a moment looking down at her face.

She was so beautiful, so gorgeous like this. My perfect little witch, aching to be taken by me.

"I want you to count," I said. "I want you to count to ten. And then after, I will take you to the bed and show you just what it means to be with an orc."

Ember nodded, turning her face so that she could look up at me.

There were tears in her eyes, but there was also lust.

Desire.

She wanted this. She wanted to be with me, to be punished. She wanted me to do whatever I wanted to her because all she wanted was to be my good little witch.

"I'm going to spank you," I said. "I'm going to spank you, and then I'm going to make you see god."

I raised the ruler again and brought it back down, smacking it right over both of her cheeks. The sound rang through the bedroom.

Ember let out a soft squeal, but it was cut off by a yelp as I spanked her again.

I paused, raising a brow expectantly.

"I thought I told you to count, Ember. I told you to count while I spanked you. Are you going to disobey me?"

"No," she whispered. She let out a little moan and then grit her teeth together. "*One.*"

I grinned down at her, warmth spreading through my chest. She was so stubborn.

"Good girl," I praised. "Such a good girl for me. You're so needy. You want me so badly."

"Yes," she rasped. "I want you to do whatever you want to me. I've wanted you since I saw you in the meeting room on Monday."

"Oh? And here I was, thinking you didn't even want me to be around you. But no, here you are, bent over my knees and ready to take whatever I give you."

"Yes," she rasped.

"Good."

I brought the ruler down again, smacking her hard. She cried out, her entire body arching. I clamped my arm over her middle back, holding her in place.

"Two!" she cried.

I brought the ruler down again, this time harder. She gasped, letting out a soft cry. One that sounded closer to tears than before.

"Three," she whispered.

I brought it down again.

"Four," she said.

And again.

"*Five!*" she cried, her voice ringing through the room.

Again.

"Six!"

Again.

"Seven!"

Again.

"*Eight.*"

Again.

"*Nine,*" she gasped, ragged.

This time I hesitated for a moment, waiting to see what she would do.

Her entire body tensed, waiting for the final spanking.

Her ass was bright red, her body racking with a soft sob. I ran my fingers lovingly over her skin, tracing the marks with the tip of my nail.

"You're such a good girl," I praised softly. "I want to hear you say it, love. I want to hear you say that you're a good girl for me, Ember."

She let out a choked sob as I swept her hair to the side. She looked up at me, her cheeks blotchy red. Tears streamed down her face, but her eyes were still swollen with that same look.

The one of desire. The one of lust.

"I'm a good girl," she whispered.

"I want you to say that you love yourself," I said.

This time, her eyes darkened.

Would she resist me? Would she refuse to say that she loved herself?

She was so precious to me. To Minni. She had no idea how much she meant to us, and the idea of her hesitating to say such a beautiful thing pained me.

She swallowed hard, and the cloud in her gaze lifted. "I love myself," she said, more tears streaming down her beautiful face. "I love myself, and I love you."

Pleasure spread through me as I fought back the tears, the burn making my throat clench.

How long had it been since I'd heard such a thing from someone? It had been so long since I confessed love to another.

I knew that I was loved. I had people in my life who cared about me who were always there for me whenever I needed them.

Even Minni. Even after all of the things that had happened to us, she was still there for me if I absolutely needed her.

"I love you too," I said.

With that, I brought the ruler down again, giving her one last spanking. I made it count, and I loved the way that her entire body took it.

I then threw the ruler to the ground, tightening my fingers around the leash. I dragged her up, pulling her into my lap.

She wrapped her arms around my neck, holding onto me. "I love you," I said again, nuzzling her. "You mean so much to me, little witch. You have no idea."

"You don't know either," she whispered.

I nodded, leaning back to look up at her. I gave her a gentle kiss and then smirked.

"Now," I said. "I'm going to make you scream again, little darling."

CHAPTER TWELVE

forgiveness

MINNI

I HAD SPENT most of the night going back and forth with myself, trying to decide if I should feel bad for the mating bond with Ember. All the while, she had slept in my bed.

I loved Ember. Just like I loved Lea.

The problem was that I had a lot of work to do with her. A lot of convincing that I wasn't sure I would be able to do.

Still, all of those worrying thoughts melted away as I watched Lea command our mate.

Ember was *ours*.

Not just mine, even though I was the only one who had a mated bond with her right now. I could see that now. I could feel how much she loved Lea. I could feel how much she wanted her through our bond, the feeling washing over me.

It reminded me of how I had felt when Lea and I first met. How I had felt about her. How I *still* felt about her.

Lea tightened her grip on the leash, drawing Ember into a hungry kiss. She moaned, leaning into our Orc mate.

If I hadn't been a vampire, my heart would have been thrashing in my chest. My blood would've been pumping in my veins, all just from watching the two of them.

My pussy throbbed as I watched them kiss, grateful that I was allowed to stay and watch.

I stood up for a moment, pulling off my clothes. The fabrics fell to the oak floors in a silky pile at my feet, my body now completely exposed.

Lea had said I could watch, but she had said nothing about me not being able to do anything to myself. I was still watching even if I was also touching myself.

I leaned back into the chair, throwing one of my legs over the arm. I spread my thighs, sliding my fingers down to my aching cunt.

Ember groaned in Lea's arms again, the two of them intertwined in a passionate kiss. I let out a soft groan as I watched them. I could feel their desires.

I was determined to have not only one mate but two now. Lea belonged to me just as much as Ember did.

Lea suddenly scooped Ember up, taking her to my bed. I watched in satisfaction as she laid her out on the duvet, pinning her arms above her head.

Ember gasped in delight, arching her body up against Lea's.

Lea leaned back for a moment, pulling her dress off and throwing it to the floor. Her entire body was naked now, her strap-on making me smirk. She'd always wielded those things with such ease.

I now had a perfect view of her breasts, of her muscles and how they rippled as she leaned down and rubbed her hands over Ember's body.

Ember let out a satisfied little gasp, her eyes wide with desire. Her scent filled the room, her heat waiting to be satiated.

Fuck. I loved watching the two of them. I bit my bottom lip, sucking in a breath.

I wanted them both. Over and over again. I could sit here for days watching them fuck, and I would never get bored.

"Please," Ember gasped. "I want you."

"I want you too," Lea moaned.

Ember bit her lower lip, spreading her legs far apart for her. Lea hovered above her, only leaning down to brush her lips over Ember's breasts. She let out a soft moan, her body glowing a little brighter.

That glow. I loved that glow.

"Come here," Lea growled, tugging on Ember's leash. She dragged her to another kiss, her growl echoing through my room.

My nipples hardened as I slid my fingers inside of me, feeling how wet I was from just watching them. I let out a little noise, followed by a soft hiss as I started to touch my clit.

I circled it slowly, waves of pleasure working through me as Lea leaned down and did the same to Ember.

Our little witch let out a soft scream, her entire body arching as if she'd been struck by lightning. I watched as the waves of need rolled through her entire body, a pleasure so strong that she could barely contain herself.

Lea pinned her back in place, forcing her to stay still.

Lea drew back, adjusting her strap-on. Her hand slid down to Ember's pussy, and she dipped two of her fingers inside of her.

Testing her, making sure she was ready to take the cock

she wore.

Ember let out a soft groan, her nipples hard, her eyes fluttering. I felt my fangs lengthen as I watched Lea position herself, placing the head of the cock against Ember's pussy.

Lea looked up, her eyes locking with mine. I arched a brow, leaning forward in my chair.

"Come here," Lea huffed. "Come watch me take her. Taste her blood as she cums for me."

"Are you sure?" I whispered, swallowing hard.

"Yes," Lea said. "I want you too."

Fuck. Why did that make my chest ache?

Ember groaned, her head tossing to the side as she looked at me.

"Please," she whispered. "I want you. I want you to hold me while I take her."

It didn't take much for me to cave into their requests. How could I deny them? How could I say no to either one of them when they looked at me like that?

"Your wish is my command, little princess," I purred.

I left my chair and went to my bed, climbing on top of it. I took the leash from Lea and tugged on it just enough to make Ember turn her head.

I wanted her to look at me as she took that cock.

"Are you going to take our orc?" I asked. "Take her cock like a good little witch?"

"Yes, My Lady," she groaned. "Please. I need it. I need it so bad."

I leaned down, our lips meeting. My fangs pricked against her bottom lip, blood welling.

A low growl left me as I tasted her.

I could taste Lea, and now I could taste Ember's blood too.

"Hold her," Lea growled.

"Yes, ma'am," I smirked, moving so that I could sit right behind Ember and pull her partially into my lap.

I reached down and caressed her breasts, pinching her nipples between my fingers.

Ember cried out as Lea moved forward, slowly pushing the head of the cock inside of her.

"You're doing so well," I said. "You do so well taking it. Such a good girl for us. Do you like being fucked by monsters?"

Ember whimpered, her little cries turning me on even more.

"Do you want to know how an orc makes a bond?" I asked

"Yes," Ember rasped. "I want to know. I want to be your mate," she said, looking only at Lea now.

"Do you want me to tell her?" I asked Lea.

"Yes," Lea whispered. "Tell our little witch just what I have to do with her to make her mine."

Lea slowly pushed her cock deeper inside Ember, making her cry out. I continued to circle her nipples with the tips of my fingers, enjoying the way her skin shivered beneath my touch.

"They have to bite you, just like I had to bite you. They have to dig their tusks into your skin and taste your blood. And then the bond starts. They have to do it with intention. The intention to love you, the intention to take you."

I leaned down closer, pressing my lips to her ear.

"She has to have the intention to keep you forever," I said softly. "Just like I intend to keep you forever."

Ember moaned as Lea pushed even deeper inside of her, her body taking another couple of inches until Lea was all the way inside of her.

Lea let out a soft groan, leaning down the steal a kiss

from Ember.

I watched the two of them gleefully, enjoying the way that Lea's tusks rubbed against Ember's soft lips.

"You feel so good," Ember moaned, breaking the kiss.

Lea chuckled, kissing down Ember's neck and then her breasts. I could still see the faint lines from the ropes I had used on her last night.

I squeezed both of her breasts, enjoying the gasp that came from her as Lea took one of them between her teeth.

Lea slowly pulled her hips back before thrusting forward, filling Ember all over again. I held her still, even as her entire body pulled against me.

"Fuck!" she cried.

"Good girl," Lea whispered. "Such a good little witch."

Ember whimpered with pleasure as she took Lea's cock over and over again. The sounds were almost enough to send me over the edge without even touching myself, her pussy wet and needy.

Lea grunted as she started to rut into her mate, fucking her harder and harder. The two of them fell into a rhythm, and I found myself lost in it.

I couldn't wait to taste Ember's blood after she'd been mated by Lea as well. I could feel my bond with her. I could *feel* what she felt.

The euphoria, the pleasure, the way she felt being taken over and over again.

"Such a good girl," Lea groaned. "Are you sure you want to take my bond?"

"Yes," Ember said, her voice almost a desperate plea. "More than anything."

The scent of her heat filled the room, the sound of Lea thrusting in and out of her making my thighs clench together.

My hands slid up her body, running over her curves all the way up to her neck.

Lea let out a soft growl, her control finally slipping free.

My eyes widened as I watched her fall into her carnal desires, finally caving and giving in to everything she wanted.

Lea leaned down once more, this time sinking her teeth into Ember's breasts.

Ember gasped, her lips parting in pain and pleasure.

I could feel the bond start to take root next to mine, the invisible lines between our souls tying us together. Binding the three of us in a way that could never be broken.

Lea's tusks dug into Ember's skin, crimson blood wetting her lips.

I ran the tip of my tongue over my fangs, the scent of her blood making me hungry.

I had thought about so many things over the past year, but I had never dreamed I'd end up here. That I would end up back with Lea, in a bed with her, with a little witch between us taking her mating bond.

One who was my mate too.

My vision blurred. I felt *happy.*

This was something Lea had wanted for so long, but she and I had never decided to do it because we were scared.

Because *I* was scared. Scared of making a life with someone. Of committing to them forever.

Forever felt different when you were immortal. When you were a creature who had been around for ages, and especially when your partner hadn't.

But, being with Ember and Lea felt right, and somehow the edge of fear had finally let go this week.

Ember let out a soft moan, her orgasm washing over her. This one was soft and lovely. Her skin started to glow a little brighter, casting a golden hue over Lea and me. It reminded me of the sun right before it set, washing over the world with its warmth.

Ember parted her lips with a soft breath, the words of the spell she had spoken to me last night tumbling from her lips.

I closed my eyes, reveling in the meaning of the words.

There were no better words to hear.

Lea slowly let go of her, running her tongue over the marks that she had left. Her eyes widened as the bond finally took root with her as well, the connection between them turning into something tangible.

"Gods," Lea breathed softly.

She pulled Ember from my arms, pulling her into her own.

My vision blurred with more tears, a single drop escaping down my face as I watched the two of them embrace.

The two of them looked so happy.

I could feel Lea's happiness, too, even though I only had a bond with Ember. It was new and lovely and bright, something the three of us would always cherish.

Three weeks ago, no one could've convinced me that I would come into an office full of monsters and witches and find my mate.

Now here I was.

Lea held on to Ember, her face resting on her shoulder. Her eyes opened, locking with my own gaze. I wiped away one of the tears quickly, not wanting her to see me cry.

Lea winked at me, her lips forming words that were not spoken aloud, but I could still read.

I forgive you.

I covered my mouth, holding back a sob.

All this time, had I really been waiting to hear her say that? Was this for everything that had happened between us? Was this forgiveness for us letting go of each other and for me taking our mate even though we agreed we would take it slowly.

Regardless, I felt it wash over me. It was like coming back to life, being forgiven by someone that I loved.

And I did love her. I loved her more than I thought possible. I loved her and Ember more than anything else in this world. I would do anything for them, anything they asked.

To the rest of the world, I was a sexy vampire who knew exactly what she wanted and exactly what to do. I was independent, rich, gorgeous, and had everything I could possibly need.

But they didn't see the cracks underneath the mask. They didn't see how much I longed to be cared for, how much I longed to be treated like everyone else.

They couldn't see that I was lonely.

Lea and Ember helped mend that void.

Ember turned around and grabbed me. I was pulled into a hug, and dragged into both of their arms. The three of us held each other on my bed, and I wasn't sure how long we sat there.

"I love you both," Ember said. "I know that it's crazy. And I know that it's sudden. But I wouldn't trade this for anything else in the world."

"I love you too, little witch," I whispered. "And you, Lea. I know that...I know that I've made mistakes. But I love you too."

Lea pulled me tighter, holding the two of us to her.

"I love you both too."

CHAPTER THIRTEEN
the interview

EMBER

I STEPPED into the office at 9 a.m. on the dot, excitement spreading through me. I was here for that promotion today. The one I had been working all year to get.

I caught a glimpse of myself in the windows of the office as I walked across the floor, attracting looks here and there from monsters and witches alike. I felt good. I looked good too. My purple hair had just been touched up, and I had added in some strips of pink too.

Today I had tied it up into two small buns looked very professional but fun. Minni had done my makeup too, dusting my eyelids with a fuchsia shimmer and giving me cat-eye liner.

I felt a flutter of butterflies as I went to the main office door.

Inferna looked up as I stepped inside, giving me a warm smile. She was always dressed well, and today was no exception. She was wearing a black blouse with a pencil skirt and heels that she could stab a monster with.

"Good morning," I chimed, grinning.

"Good morning," Inferna said, smiling back. She stood up from her desk, coming around to meet me. "Are you ready for your interview with the big boss?"

"Yes," I said, taking a deep breath. I was trying not to be too nervous, but it was hard.

"You're going to do great," she chuckled. "You've been working so hard to get this. You've studied all the things you need to know, and you've been leading a solid team."

"Thank you," I said. "I've learned from the best."

Art seemed to appear from nowhere, giving me a soft smile from the corner of the room. "You're going to be great," he said. "But just make sure you don't bring up anything about his tail."

Tail? "Whose tail?" I asked, a wave of confusion washing over me.

"The boss," he said. "He gets self-conscious about it sometimes."

I stared at him for a moment, frowning.

His expression changed, becoming overly friendly. "You're going to do great, Ember. Go ahead and go upstairs. You don't want to be late."

I gave them both a little nod, giving Inferna a quick hug before leaving the office. I crossed back over the floor, my shoes clacking over the linoleum. Morning light poured in from the windows, spring blooming outside.

Everything was absolutely perfect.

I went past the front desk, giving Anne a smile. She gave me a happy wave, and a wink as well.

I paused for a moment before stepping back out towards the elevator. I took a deep breath, steeling myself.

This was gonna work out. I was going to make my sibling very proud of me. I was going to make everyone very proud of me.

I went to the elevator and hit the button to go to the next floor, waiting patiently for the doors to slide open. They opened with a ding, and I stepped inside.

They closed behind me, leaving me alone. I hit the button for the next floor and then took another deep breath. Trying to calm myself, trying to control the butterflies within my stomach. I was so nervous, but I knew the moment I started talking in the interview that I would do great.

When I was hired on, it had been... What had it been?

I frowned as the elevator lifted me, my stomach lurching. I couldn't remember what it had been like before I was hired.

I didn't have too long to think, because the doors opened again and I was delivered to the next floor where the boss waited.

I was perfectly on time, and as I stepped out, I felt a breath of relief. I moved down the hall, crossing the floor to where his office was.

I went to the doorway, giving the door a soft knock.

"Ember," his booming voice chimed.

I took a peek inside, seeing the monster himself seated at his opulent desk. The walls had been painted a deep turquoise and were decorated with different certificates and awards. There was a massive TV screen on the wall, one that he used when he was doing his meetings with us. There had been jokes around the office before that all he did was sit upstairs and watch TV all day, but I knew that wasn't true.

Alfred was a hard worker. He had earned to be where he was. He had done so much for us, especially for me.

My smile faltered, the thought sticking with me. Was that true? *Had* he done a lot for me?

The thoughts melted away as I stepped into the office.

"Good morning, Alfred," I said.

Alfred looked like a werewolf, although his form sometimes changed into something more dragon-like. He wore a very nice suit, his snout pulled back into a fanged smile.

The way his eyes were pinned on me made me feel sick for a moment. But that was nerves, right?

"How are you doing today?" he asked.

He stood from his desk, his form towering over mine. He was massive, his shoulders wide, his muscles bulky even beneath the suit. His form shimmered for a moment, showing me scales and an even more wicked grin before going back to his wolven self.

He came around the desk, his tail dragging behind him.

"I'm doing well," I said through my teeth. "I'm excited to interview."

"Excellent," he said. "It'll be a quick one. It really is just a formality. You come with great recommendations, and I've heard nothing but good things. We like to promote people from within the company who deserve it."

All of the little alarm bells in my mind were smoothed over with his warm words.

Alfred held out his clawed hand, and I took it, giving it a gentle shake. A stab of electricity shot through my arm, the panic flaring back up.

I did my best to make sure he couldn't tell that I was truly nervous. *What was going on?*

Alfred held on to my hand, giving me another toothy grin.

"It's interesting," he said. "All this time you spent running from me. Running from everything you were born to do. But here we are, and you're doing just fine. You even look happy."

What did he mean? What did he mean I'd been running?

I pulled my hand from his, placing it on my side. I did my best to mask my concern, plastering over his weird words with a fake smile. "What do you mean?"

"Don't worry about it," he chuckled.

He gave me one more look before turning and moving back around to his desk. He pulled out his chair and took a seat. The energy of the room seemed to change, melting into something that felt *different*.

I looked back up at the TV, swallowing hard. It looked blurry for a moment, flickering on and then off.

My brain felt fuzzy, my heart hammering in my chest.

I was here to interview, I reminded myself. Here to interview for a promotion...

But what promotion was it?

"Take a seat," Alfred said, gesturing at the chair in front of his desk.

I didn't hesitate, immediately moving to the chair. I took a seat, spreading my hands over my slacks to wipe the sweat away.

"So," Alfred said. "What do you know about witches? Specifically, omega witches?"

"Omega witches?" I asked, puzzled. Those didn't exist, nor had they ever. Within the world of creatures, there were omegas, but not for witches.

"Those don't exist," I said.

Was this some sort of test?

"I mean, within the world of monsters and creatures, of

course, there are omegas. But witches have never had them. We don't have alphas, we don't have betas, we don't have mating bites or anything like that. But I'm not really sure this is something we should be talking about at work."

"And why not?" Alfred asked, giving me an incredulous look.

"Well, I'm here for an interview for work. And working here has nothing to do with omegas. Or with omega witches even existing."

"I suppose. *But,*" he said, tapping his claws on the desktop. "I'm the boss. And I would like to talk about this a little bit more before we get started on our interview. Because I'm curious. I'm curious as to how long it will take you before you recall what's really happening. I knew my magic was good after everything, but I didn't think it was this good."

I felt that flutter of disturbance again, the nerves working through me.

I felt my magic stirring, buzzing in my veins. That only happened when there was a threat, but I was safe here.

It was just another day at the office. It was just another day for Warts & Claws Inc.

"Is Alex here?" I asked suddenly.

"Alex?" Alfred asked, leaning forward. "Alex who?"

Alex...

Who was he, anyway?

My head ached for a moment, straining against all of these thoughts that I had no answers to. All of these questions suddenly plagued me, and yet the only thing that I could think about was getting this goddamn job.

I looked up at Alfred, holding his gaze. We stared at each other for a minute until something finally clicked. It was like the last piece of the puzzle slid into place, and suddenly I felt fear.

Sweat immediately beaded on the back of my neck, a chill icing my spine. Still, I did my best not to televise my feelings. I masked everything that I felt, hiding away all of those fears that something else was happening.

Something else *was* happening. Fuck.

"Do you have any interview questions for me?" I asked, trying to redirect him.

I was remembering things left and right now. This wasn't real. This couldn't be real. I had never wanted a promotion here. I was still new to the office, and the work was fine, but being a boss here? That had never been on my agenda.

But that was on his agenda. His agenda was to destroy me and every other witch in the office that was an omega.

"Sure," he said, his voice lightening up. He was going to play along with it for now. "First question. Tell me, what is your greatest strength?"

I wanted to tell him that destroying fear demons was my greatest strength. Now that everything was suddenly coming back to me, I knew I could use some things to my advantage. And maybe even get some information. Information that no one else had.

But also, this was dangerous. How in the hell was he in my dreams?

Was this a dream?

"One of my greatest strengths is my determination," I said. "Once I set my mind on something, I never give up."

Alfred chuckled. "I think we might be similar in that way."

I fought the urge to scoff, bile rising in my throat. I didn't want to be compared to him.

"Can you tell me about a time you disagreed with someone in the workplace and how you resolved it?"

I could see by the twinkle in his eyes that he knew what he was asking. I stared at him and then nodded pleasantly.

"Of course," I said.

I took a deep breath, shifting in my seat. My fingertips started to burn with magic, aching to be set free. It was like wildfire when it wanted to be used.

Fuck it. I had to get out of this. How the hell was I going to wake up?

"Well, you see. I once worked with a boss, someone who was very mean. Someone who was downright evil. And he believed he was entitled to whatever he wanted. And that others should suffer for it."

"Oh dear," Alfred said, a smile teasing his lips. "Sounds dreadful."

"Very dreadful," I said. I leaned forward in my seat, arching my brow. "You see, he really believed that he was the best boss. And that he was going to win. But he wasn't. He would never win."

His smile became poisoned, his expression one that made my stomach feel sick. "Ah, I see. I think you remember now, don't you?"

I leaned back in my seat. There was no point in hiding anything now. "I do. What the fuck are you doing in my head? And why are you messing with my dreams?"

"Well. I came here to give you a message. To make sure you understand something," Alfred said as if it were the nicest thing in the world.

"Understand what?" I growled.

My magic continued to itch. It was the kind of magic that gave light and warmth, but it could also be dangerous.

When Cinder and I had been abandoned, they had made sure I knew how to fight. Even though Cinder had always been the one to fight the battles, they still showed me how to use my magic for defense.

I had to learn how to do that because of the bastard who was sitting in front of me.

He had hurt Cinder. He had hurt me. He had hurt so many others.

This cycle of destruction needed to end.

"I want you to come to the office," Alfred said simply. He leaned forward, propping his chin up on his clawed hand. "I want you to come to work. I want you to come see me. I want you to finally give yourself over to me, or everyone else will suffer. I will ruin Cinder's pretty new life. I will make sure Inferna and Calen, and Art all suffer. Even Billy and his mates. I will make sure that I tear down every single one of the people in the office that you've come to care about, and I will make sure that they wish for their death. They don't know. They have no idea what I have waiting for them. Especially for little Alex. Alex, thinking he is immune to all of this. Thinking he can escape me? No. He will never escape me. He brought me here, and he belongs to me. First, I need magic. I need your magic, Ember. So," Alfred growled, leaning forward even more. "What's it going to be?"

Even though his words sent a chill down my spine, and even though I was now trembling in my seat, I refused to show weakness in front of this monster. This monster who had destroyed so many lives, who thought he would be able to hurt all of us. He would touch no one, and he would hurt no one who belonged to me.

"I'm going to destroy you," I whispered.

Alfred let out a booming laugh, leaning back in his chair before standing up. He slammed his hands down on the desk, the entire room shaking. All of his office supplies spilled over, falling to the floor.

I jumped to my feet, magic immediately bursting from my hands. I glowed now, turning the room gold.

This is a dream, I reminded myself. Nothing but a dream. A nightmare. But still, even though he was a demon, I was still a witch. I was still a witch, and I was still in control.

The lights flickered overhead, a low growl echoing through the entire room. The two of us stared at each other, like two creatures squaring off to fight. I could feel my magic growing stronger now, aching to release. Aching to take out revenge on this monster who had done so many terrible things to everyone.

"Come to the office," Alfred said, his nails digging into the wood of the desk. "Come to the office by Friday, or I will start with your new mates. You think you're so safe from me. You think you're safe because you're at your new precious home. But it didn't take much to find out where your vampire mate lives. It wasn't very hard at all. If you do not come to the office, and if you do not do so without telling anyone where you are going, I will make sure you live to regret it for the rest of your life."

"Get the fuck out of my dreams!" I screamed.

Alfred picked up the desk, throwing it to the side. I moved back just as it collided with the wall, the windows shattering.

He lunged for me, but I fell back into my magic. Letting it completely engulf me with its warmth, and its protection.

This was *my* dream. This was my space.

Alfred managed to grab me by the neck, squeezing tightly. He leaned in, his foul breath making me feel sick to my stomach.

"If you don't come to the office, everyone you love will die."

With those hateful words growled, his entire body suddenly went up into smoke, the dream finally ending.

The interview was over. Needless to say, I had not gotten that promotion.

CHAPTER FOURTEEN

forget

LEA

I SHOOK MY MATE AWAKE, feeling her fear spread through me. Minni also shook her, letting out a string of curses.

Ember's eyes finally flew open, and she looked lost. I hated that expression, and I hated knowing that whatever had just happened, I hadn't been able to pull her out of it.

The three of us had decided to have an afternoon nap, which had gone terribly wrong. Within about 30 minutes of Ember being asleep, she started whimpering. She sounded like she was in pain, and no matter how hard Minni and I tried to wake her up, she wouldn't.

"Oh my god, are you okay?" Minni gasped, grabbing her shoulders.

Ember nodded, letting out a deep breath. She was shaken up, her body trembling.

"Ember," I whispered. "Are you sure you're okay? What

just happened? We've been trying to wake you up for a few minutes now, but you would not wake up."

I gripped her shoulders, giving her a slight shake.

"He came to my dreams," Ember said softly. "It felt like it was just another day at the office. But it was different. I was there for an interview for a big promotion. I even saw Inferna and Art. And then I went upstairs, and Alex wasn't the boss. Alfred was."

"Did he hurt you?" Minni asked, letting out a low hiss. She bared her fangs, her anger leaking through the room.

I was doing my best to keep calm, but I was infuriated. The fact was that bastard had invaded her dreams, and we couldn't stop it. Not only was I angry, but I was also worried that it would happen again.

What if he was able to hurt her while she was in her dreams? What if he was able to kill her? To take her magic?

I was just an orc. Minni was just a vampire. Neither of us had any special abilities when it came to the mind, especially when it came to magic. We were relatively simple monsters, and that was not where our strengths were.

"He didn't hurt me," Ember said. "He was very threatening. He told me that he was going to hurt everyone. He told me that I *had* to come to the office."

"Well, there's no way in hell that's happening," Minni growled. "Over my dead body."

"You're already dead," I said, earning a dirty look from her. "But still. You're not going anywhere. Not in this weather, it's still snowing outside, and it's enough to where traveling isn't safe. The storm hasn't let up and won't until tomorrow morning. So at least for the time being, you're still stuck with us," I said.

Ember pressed her lips together, not pleased with that answer. Which didn't make me feel good either.

"What else did he say?" Minni asked, her shoulders finally relaxing some.

"He was trying to... It's like he was interviewing me. And he was playing with me. He wanted to see how long it would take until I remembered what was really happening. At first, I didn't realize I was in a dream. Everything felt so real. But then I realized I couldn't remember what the promotion was for, and then I started remembering other things, and then I remembered everything. But... aside from throwing the desk into the wall and grabbing me by the neck, he didn't hurt me. He just threatened me. He said if I didn't go, everyone would get hurt."

I didn't like the way she said that. There was hesitance in her voice, and I could already see the wheels in her head turning. Was she really thinking about going to the office after everything that had happened? Was she really thinking I would allow her to go there, knowing she was in heat and that monster wanted her?

There was no way in hell that was going to happen. Minni and I would fight to the death on that.

"Everyone is in danger," Ember whispered.

"Everyone will be in more danger if you decide to do something stupid," Minni said. "You have to think this through. And plus, Lea is correct. None of us is getting out of this house at least until tomorrow, and maybe then we can plan to stop him."

Ember nodded mutely, leaning against me. I held her in my arms for a few moments, letting her warmth spread through me. It didn't matter that it was snowing outside, not when I had a little witch right here in my arms.

Our bonds were still new, but I could feel so much. And I could feel Minni too. I liked that.

I pressed my nose to the top of her head, breathing in her scent. At the same time, I held Minni's gaze.

She was just as frazzled as me now, the two of us thinking about how we couldn't reach Ember. It had been a nightmare.

"It'll be okay," Ember said.

She clutched me a little tighter and then looked up, her eyes wide. I cupped her face, leaning down and brushing my lips across hers. She let out a soft little moan, and all of my worries seemed to melt at once. It was hard to focus when one of my mates was in heat.

"I want to forget," Ember whispered, looking back at Minni too.

I let out a groan, running my fingers through my hair. "You just scared the hell out of both of us, and now you want us to fuck you?"

"Yes," Ember giggled. "Sorry, now that I'm awake, I'm very horny."

"Well, what are we going to do about that?" Minni asked.

Minni reached out, tangling her talons in Ember's hair, yanking her head back. She stole a deep kiss, drawing out a moan from our mate.

Our mate.

It would take me a while to get used to thinking that.

Still...

Ember seemed to be okay, and now I was desperate to make her forget the nightmare she had just survived.

She was still in heat and desperate for release. How could I be a good mate if I didn't help her out?

"Tie her up," I said, giving Minni a knowing look. "I want to make her forget for a little while."

"Yes, ma'am," Minni said, smirking.

"I will be back," I said. "With all of the fun things."

Ember's eyes brightened, a smile spreading across her face. "This will be fun."

"It will be, little witch. For all three of us."

CHAPTER FIFTEEN
lipstick stains

MINNI

I COULDN'T FIGHT off the excited laugh as I led Ember down to a different room in the house. I had one in each of my homes because I had particular tastes.

I could hear Ember's heart pounding as I pushed her into the room.

"Undress," I commanded.

I turned on one of the lights, casting a soft amber glow over us. This room was my dungeon. Each house I had always had a dungeon because I liked to play.

Ember's clothing fell to the floor, and she turned to look at me, arching her brow. I stood for a moment, admiring her. I traced her curves with my gaze, touching the tip of one of my fangs with my tongue.

I hungered for her.

"Beautiful," I whispered. "You're stunning, Ember. There's a very real part of me that wants to devour you right now."

I stepped up to her, running the back of my finger over her nipples. They perked up, her breath hitching.

I swept her violet hair back, leaning in to press my lips against the curve of her neck. I left a lipstick stain, marking her as *mine*.

I kissed her cheek, leaving another mark.

"Stay right here," I breathed.

Ember nodded, dragging in a breath to try and steady herself.

"Tell me what you want, little witch," I whispered. "Do you want me to tie you up? Do you want to be helpless in front of your monsters?"

"Yes," she whispered.

The flutter of her heart turned me on. I let out a soft growl, a pleased one.

I wondered what Lea had in mind for her. Regardless, I knew what I wanted.

"You're going to look beautiful," I said, smirking. "I'm going to suspend you up in the air. And if at any point you feel uncomfortable, please let us know. Please make sure to use your safe-word if you need it. Also, if at any point, any of your body parts start to feel tingly, numb or like they are in pain, you must tell us. At that point, we will cut you down."

"You're going to tie me up in the air?"

"Yes," I said. "I want you helpless and in need. Our little damsel in distress."

Ember's eyes brightened, her skin flushing. "I would love that."

"Good," I said. "I will be back. I want you to rub your clit while I go get everything."

"Yes, My Lady," she said.

She slid her hand down to her pussy. I swallowed hard

as she began to rub her clit, her immediate gasp telling me just how sensitive she was right now.

I went and grabbed my rope kit. Within a few minutes, I returned with three fifty feet bundles of violet hemp rope, shears, and everything that I needed to suspend her in the air.

When I came back into the room, she was still rubbing her clit. Her eyes were glazed over, a moan leaving her.

I went to her and pulled her hand away, bringing her fingers up to my lips. "Good girl," I whispered, kissing them. "Arms up, little witch."

Ember immediately lifted her arms, and I readied the rope, taking a step closer to her. I started with her torso, enjoying the way the rope ran across her skin. The vibrations felt good on my fingertips.

"I like how that feels," she whispered.

"The vibrations?"

"Yes," she said, shivering.

I was going to tie her completely this time, and I couldn't wait until she was bound in the air, helpless and crying out.

Ember closed her eyes, her body relaxing as I did my work. I took my time, pausing to kiss her neck, play with her breasts, or run my nails down her back.

I left scarlet kiss marks as I went, marking her over and over as mine.

"How does this feel?" I asked.

"It feels good," she huffed.

I smiled to myself, continuing my work. I began to make the knots, looping the rope across each other, creating a harness. One of my favorite things about chest harnesses was when it was around beautiful breasts, squeezing them ever so slightly.

I could hear her heart, the beat becoming a rhythm in my own body as I bound her.

"I can't wait to taste you," I murmured, tightening more of the ropes around her body. Some of the ropes went across her stomach, down to her hips, wrapping around her thighs. I made the patterns, enjoying how she looked.

I positioned her arms above her head after binding them, creating a point I could suspend from.

I turned her around and paused, biting my lower lip as I looked at her ass. I reached down, giving her a slap.

"I just had to make sure your ass was still slappable."

She giggled, grinning. "Thanks."

This was perfect.

Everything about *her* was perfect, from the color of her hair, to how soft her skin was to how stunning she looked tied up. She was beautiful, and she was mine.

Lea came back into the room finally, bringing a whole slew of items that she was going to use to play with our mate

.

I reached up, grabbing the connection to the suspending system. I had tested it earlier to make sure everything was good.

I brought the clip down to the rope around her wrists and arms, attaching it. I gave it a hard tug and then took a step back, admiring my work.

"How do I look?" Ember asked.

"Halfway to being helpless," I chuckled.

I reached down, pulling on the rope that I had wrapped around one of her thighs, bringing her leg up. She hobbled for a moment, her balance thrown off.

"Relax," I hissed. "You can trust the ropes. You can start to pull on them, give it all of your whole weight. You're already suspended from your arms and are safe. And soon, you'll be suspended from this point as well."

Ember nodded, her eyes wide as she slowly relaxed. She let out a nervous breath, but at least her heartbeat started to calm.

"Good girl," I praised.

It didn't take much longer, and soon I had her completely tied. She was suspended now, her body waiting to be touched. I had one of her legs correct at an angle, the suspension point around her knee. While I had her other leg bent so that the suspension point was from her ankle. Now she was completely tied and unable to get away from her monstrous mates.

"These feel good," Ember whispered.

I could see that she was starting to slip into subspace, her eyes becoming softer. Her voice was gentle and soothed, her muscles finally relaxing.

"Good," I said. Circling my work. "They should feel good. They should feel safe."

Lea made a noise of approval, circling her as well. "This is perfect," Lea said. "Our little mate is all tied up."

"She is," I purred, "Our little damsel in distress."

I traced the tip of my nail over her soft skin, breathing in her scent. I pressed my lips against the crook of her neck, breathing her in.

Ember shivered, her heart pounding a little faster.

"I'm going to do so many things to you," I whispered.

I brought my nails down her chest, tracing one of the veins that was becoming more prominent all the way down to her breasts. The ropes squeezed both of them, her nipples hard and sensitive.

"Who do you belong to, little witch?"

"You," she gasped. "My Lady."

"Do you want us to save you, little witch? Save you from your burning heat?"

"Please," she begged. "Please. I can't escape it. You're the only one who can help."

Her words sent a thrill through me.

Lea moved behind her, giving me a dark look over her shoulders. We smirked at each other, and for once, I was thankful that I knew her. She was easy to read, especially in moments like this.

I leaned forward, dragging the tip of my tongue down her chest. I took one of her nipples between my lips, sucking it gently.

Lea knelt behind her, her hands gripping Ember's thigh and hip as she began to eat her out.

Her scent made me hungry. I wanted to drink from her, to taste her blood and pussy.

"Oh fuck," Ember moaned.

She tried jerking against the ropes, and I looked up just as her expression of realization hit.

She wasn't going anywhere.

I smiled, my fangs lengthening. I ran the tip of my tongue over her nipple again, teasing her.

She let out a string of curses, her head falling back with a groan.

"Fuck, both of you are driving me crazy," she moaned.

"Good," I said.

With a possessive growl, I sank my fangs into her breast. Ember let out a scream, one that ended in a groan.

The taste of her blood filled my mouth, and the hunger that I had been fighting since meeting her raised its head.

I moaned, drinking more. The sound of her heartbeat and blood dripping into my mouth drowned out the sound of her cries and groans. I knew Lea was playing with her, teasing her, getting her ready for whatever we wanted to do next— but all I could think about was consuming her. Breathing in her very essence, devouring her soul.

I could feel our bonds, could feel her pleasure at giving in to us.

Finally, I found a shred of restraint and drew back. Two lines of blood dripped from the punctures, rolling down her breast. I leaned down, licking it up with the tip of my tongue.

"Again," she gasped. "Fuck. Please."

A low growl left me, and I kissed further down her body, this time biting her hip. She let out a sharp gasp again before melting into it.

Fuck. I could taste her pleasure, could taste how her blood was getting sweeter and sweeter. I looked up as I drank, watching as Lea kissed her neck and teased her.

I pulled my fangs out again, kissing further until I was on my knees in front of her pussy.

She was already so fucking wet for us.

Lea had joked about me taking blood from Ember's clit, but I was going to.

I pressed my lips against her pussy, licking her clit. Circling it with my tongue. She gasped, trying to move even though she was tied in place.

Lea let out a dark chuckle. "I like the way you writhe, little lady. Especially when our vampire is doing such naughty things to you."

I pushed two of my fingers inside of her, thrusting them as I lapped at her.

She screamed, her pussy convulsing around me. She was getting so close to cumming, so close to coming undone just for me.

I wanted her to cum on my lips, and then I wanted to take my meal.

"Please don't stop," she cried, her voice ragged.

Lea's arms wrapped around her, and I looked up, watching as her arm came around her neck.

"Please," she gasped, sucking in the air just as Lea started to slowly cut it off.

She instantly became wetter. I pulled my lips free and rubbed her clit, moving my fingers quickly.

As Lea let go of her, she let out a gasp, her body arching against the ropes as her first orgasm crashed into her.

I leaned forward as she came, eager to taste her. I drove my tongue inside of her, lapping up everything. I then moved back up, sucking on her clit.

She screamed, and I knew I could make her cum again. I didn't stop, wanting to drive her straight back to the edge.

She tried to form words, but they were lost in a groan as her entire body answered me. She came again, another orgasm wracking her.

In one swift motion, I used the tip of my fang to pierce her and started drinking her blood again.

She barely noticed the pain, immediately drawn into more and more pleasure. I groaned as I tasted her, reveling in the beauty of her blood. It was sweet and full of passion and love and *fuck*.

I closed my eyes with a soft moan, focusing on our bond together.

My mate. I loved her, wanted her, and was desperate for her. She was beautiful and kind and mine.

"I can't again!" she gasped, but I knew she could.

"Of course, you can," Lea growled. "Cum for us again, little lady."

Ember made a noise, her body trembling. Lea knelt

down behind her, slowly pressing two of her fingers inside of her as I drank from her.

Ember's moans became more and more urgent, the scent of her heat engulfing me. I groaned, knowing she was so close.

Lea began to thrust her fingers in and out faster, going and going until finally— our mate let out a scream.

I finished tasting her and sat back, taking everything in. Lea was kissing her, wiping away the tears that strolled down her cheeks just like the drops of blood dripped down her skin from where I had marked her.

I smirked, licking my lips in satisfaction.

"Beautiful," I whispered. "A little golden goddess."

Her cheeks flushed, her lips tugging into a satisfied smile. "I want to do things to both of you," she whispered.

"You will," Lea said. "You will do all of the things, but right now, this is about you. And about making you cum over and over again. About breaking your heat and trying new things."

She let out a little mewl but didn't argue.

I licked my lips again, basking in the taste of her.

Lea met my gaze over her shoulder, arching a brow. "And besides. I think Minni wants to try out her riding crop."

"Yes," Ember said.

"Demanding orc," I teased, standing up.

Lea only smiled. "Make her cum again, vamp."

"So cocky," I hissed, but I still found myself going to the small table that I had laid things out on. "Get her down, but keep her arms tied."

"Sure," Lea said. "As you wish."

I fought the urge to stick my tongue out at her and studied all of the items on the table. I selected a riding crop and a blindfold, thinking about exactly what I wanted to do next.

She'd enjoyed being spanked, and I'd enjoyed how red her ass had been under Lea's hand.

Now, I wanted to put her on the floor and spank her. Play with her. Tease her. Edge her and warm her up until she was begging again.

And then, once I'd made her cum again, I'd see what Lea wanted to do to me.

I went back to Lea and Ember, watching as Lea lowered her to the floor and untied some of the ropes.

"I really love the ropes," Ember said. "They're freeing. It's ironic."

"There's something about being tied up," I agreed, smirking. "For me, it's the closest I ever get to going straight into subspace. Which is hard to do."

"I imagine you always as a dominant," Ember giggled.

"Well," I said, leaning down to steal a kiss from her. "When it comes to you, sweetheart, I certainly like doing things to you."

Lea pulled the last knot free, leaving out our witch's arms still bound but the rest of her body free.

"On your knees, princess," I said.

Ember made a noise but obeyed, kneeling in front of me. My eyes traced over the lines from the ropes, the slight indentions satisfying.

I brought the riding crop up, placing it under her chin. I tilted her face up, leaning in closer.

"Open your mouth, little slut," I commanded.

Her eyes flashed for a moment, and I wondered if she would use her safe-word. I waited patiently, waiting to see what she was comfortable with.

Her lips parted, her heartbeat growing louder. I watched as her skin flushed, a little moan leaving her.

"Wider, little slut," I said.

She parted them wider.

I leaned forward and spit, watching as it hit her tongue.

"Swallow," I said.

She obeyed like a good little witch.

"Good girl," I said. "Such a good little slut for us, aren't you?"

"Yes, My lady," she whispered.

That made me smile. "Good. Now up. Stand and follow me."

Lea arched a brow, curious as to what I would do. Ember stood, and I held out my hand, turning and pulling her behind me. I led her to another chaise that was on the far side of the room.

I pushed her onto the chaise, putting her on her knees on the cushion.

"Hands on the wall," I said. "Lean against the back of the chaise."

She obeyed again perfectly.

Now, her ass faced me, and she was in the perfect position for me to tease her.

Lea took a seat next to her, leaning back so that she'd be able to watch.

I stuck my tongue out at her, drawing a chuckle from her.

Ember let out a breath, her muscles trembling with anticipation.

I dragged the end of the riding crop down her spine, teasing her. I traced her body, running it over the curve of her ass and thighs.

"Such a good little slut," I said. "Aren't you? So eager to please us."

"Yes, My Lady," she whispered.

"You just want to get used over and over again."

"Yes," she breathed.

"You just want to cum until there's not a single thought left in your head."

"Yes."

Good.

This was going to be fun.

CHAPTER SIXTEEN
throwback thursday

EMBER

MINNI BROUGHT the riding crop down, the pain coming and quickly fading. I gasped, biting my lower lip with a moan.

She and Lea had already made me cum three times, but that wasn't enough. They wanted me to cum again, to truly make me fall apart.

Fuck. I closed my eyes, feeling the pleasure through the bonds. They loved seeing me like this as much as I loved being like this.

I was mated to a vampire and an orc and loved every single thing about that.

She brought the crop down again, this time over my ass. I gasped, only for her to spank me with it again. And again.

I was wet. I was so fucking wet, the pain becoming something that turned me on more and more.

"Please," I groaned.

"Please, what?" Lea asked. "You have to be specific when you're begging her."

I looked over at her, holding her honey gaze. I loved it when she was like this— when she had a wicked edge to her words.

"Please spank me again," I rasped.

"Louder," Lea said.

Fuck. I blushed, feeling a little embarrassed.

Minni snorted. "You're embarrassed now of all times? After I've had blood from your pussy, and tied you up? Lea's put you on a leash and has fucked you senseless."

"Sorry, My Lady," I whispered.

She laughed, the sound sending a chill down my spine.

"Such a little slut, and she wants to suddenly be modest."

Her words made me even wetter, and I couldn't stop myself from letting out a little moan.

Minni struck my ass again, drawing a yelp from me.

She hit my other cheek. Again, and then again. Each time, drawing a gasp or cry from me.

Finally, she tossed it to the side and ran her hands down my back. Her fingers knotted in my hair, and she yanked my head to the side, leaning forward to kiss me.

She left me breathless and then slid her arms around my body, her fingers sliding down to my pussy.

Fuck. Her touch alone sent me spiraling, her low growl turning me on even more.

"Please," I gasped. "Please let me cum."

"Let you?" Minni purred. "Sure, sweetheart, I will let you cum. You've been so good for me."

She started to rub my clit in quick circles, drawing a cry from me. My legs trembled as I did my best not to collapse forward.

"Cum for me," she growled.

Fuck. Her voice was a sultry snarl, her command sending me straight over the edge.

I closed my eyes, seeing stars as another orgasm crashed into me. I let go of everything, allowing it to take me completely.

Minni held me, kissing the side of my neck.

"Gods," I whispered.

I could barely think. I opened my eyes.

Hell, I could barely see.

Minni slowly let go, only for Lea to pull me into her lap. She ran her fingers through my hair, and I closed my eyes, relaxing against her.

Within a few moments, I was fast asleep.

I SAT STRAIGHT UP in bed, looking around in the darkness. Minni and Lea were in bed, too, both asleep.

I took in a breath, steadying myself.

Another dream. I'd had another dream about Alfred.

Which sucked because I'd fallen asleep after four mind-shattering orgasms. You'd think that would be enough to make my dreams out of commission.

I swallowed hard, my thoughts reeling.

I had to go to him.

He was going to hurt everyone if I didn't. And I knew that he wasn't lying.

I was running out of time.

Fuck.

My magic buzzed at my fingertips, and I held my hands up, silently mouthing a spell for stealth. One that would let me sneak out without waking them, although I wasn't sure if I even needed it.

I looked at Lea and then Minni and carefully crawled out of bed. They were both passed out.

I left the bedroom, my heart pounding.

Fuck. I had no choice.

I knew that I shouldn't do it, but I still got dressed and slipped out of the house before the sun even rose. The storm had finally let up, and the snow crunched underfoot as I went to Lea's car.

I knew that they were going to be mad at me, but I had to go to the office. I had to make sure that everyone was going to be safe.

I could handle him. I knew that I could fight him. Maybe if I could stop him, everyone would finally be able to let go of everything that had been happening here at this office.

I got into the car, turning over the engine. Within a few moments, I was able to back out of the driveway and hit the road, speeding towards the office.

It didn't take very long for me to get there. Because the sun had yet to rise, there was no traffic, and the world was still quiet around us. The city streets were damn near empty, almost eerily so.

I pulled into the parking garage, checking my phone as I stole a spot. I sent a text message to Lea and Minni, letting them know what I had decided to do.

I knew they were going to be angry, but again. I had to do this. I had no other choice.

Everything was going to be okay, though. I knew that it was. Even if he ended up taking me back, everyone else would be safe, and that was all that mattered.

I pulled my coat around me tightly, looking in my rearview mirror at the parking garage. There was only one car, one I didn't recognize but was on.

I stared at it for a moment, and then I opened up my door. I stepped out of the car, slamming it shut behind me. The crisp air sent goosebumps over my skin, and I found myself pulling my coat and scarf even closer to my body.

My footsteps echoed through the parking garage as I went towards the car, pausing when I was only a few feet away from it. I could feel the eyes from behind the dark glass staring at me. Watching me.

The door slowly opened and out stepped someone who I had never met before.

A woman. Or, maybe not a woman, based on how her eyes glowed. She arched a brow, her expression radiating rage.

"So you have finally come?" She sniffed, glaring at me.

"Yes," I said. "I expected Alfred to be here, not whoever you are."

"I'm his assistant," she said. "His most loyal servant."

"Okay then," I said. What the hell was I supposed to do with that? I was expecting Alfred to show up. Not his servant. Now what?

"You're just like your sibling," she said, scowling. "Thinking you'll be able to work your way out of this. Come with me, get in the car quietly, and if you try anything stupid, it will be the death of you."

Fuck.

I wish I knew what she was. Maybe I would be able to fight her. Still...

"I'm not going with you," I said. "Alfred was going to meet me here. And I expect Alfred to be the one to take me. Not you. I don't care who you are, but I will not go with you. That was not the agreement."

"What agreement?" She snarled, taking a step forward.

"It's really none of your business," I said. "Confidential."

"You either get in the car," she said, her voice dropping low. "Or everything that Alfred promised would happen if you did not come will happen."

Her voice was unwavering, the threat real.

I glanced around the parking garage willing more time, looking directly at the security cameras that I knew were watching. Always watching. I could only hope that everyone would be able to see what happened to me and that they would be able to find me.

By the time they found me, I wanted this whole situation to be able to be put behind us. I wanted Alfred to be back in hell and for the snotty assistant to be forgotten.

I didn't say anything, but I did cross the rest of the parking garage to the car. I opened up the passenger door, climbing inside. With a little hiss, Alfred's assistant climbed into the driver's side and slammed the door shut behind her. All the locks activated, the clicking noise echoing through the cabin.

"Is that really necessary?" I asked, looking at her. "I'm already here. Willingly."

"I don't trust you," she said, turning on the car. "And I don't want to hear another word out of your mouth for the rest of the road trip."

I was about to argue, but her hand touched my shoulder. I felt a surge of darkness run through me, and all of my magic immediately snuffed out. My vision started to blur, spots of darkness overtaking everything.

Within a few moments, I fell into darkness.

WHEN I OPENED MY EYES, I was sitting in an office not much different from the one that I had been working in. The only difference was this time, the lights were flickering, some of the glass was broken, and I was tied down to a chair.

There was a massive desk in front of me, one that had an even larger chair behind it. And in that chair was the beast who had been haunting my nightmares in my life for years now.

"Alfred," I growled.

Somehow, sitting in front of him now, I didn't feel a lick of fear. I had been waiting for this moment for so long, hoping that I would be able to do something. And even though I was tied up, my magic wasn't gone. Whatever his assistant had done, it hadn't lasted long.

But maybe that was his intention. I wasn't sure yet, but I would find out.

"Ember," Alfred said, his eyes pinned on me.

He looked even angrier than he had in my dreams. He had the body of a werewolf, his massive head ending in a snout with fangs. He wore a nice button-down, slacks, and a navy tie. If it weren't for the fact that he had a dragon's tail and that when he sometimes growled, fire would flicker from his lips, he might've just come across as a normal monster working at the office.

But I knew better.

I knew better than to think this monster was a normal one. Less than a month ago, I had fought a fear demon he had put in my mind. Then he had put it in my friends' minds. He had done so many things to hurt others, including imprisoning omega witches and using their power for himself.

He had hurt monsters, he had hurt witches, and he had hurt people who I loved. And I knew that he wouldn't stop.

"I did what you said," I growled. "I came. I didn't tell

anyone that I was meeting you. And now you will leave them alone, just as you promised."

"Indeed," Alfred said, his voice a rumble that echoed through the room. He stood up from his desk, his chair's legs screeching against the floor.

"What do you want?" I asked.

"You," Alfred said, coming around the desk to stop in front of my chair.

He towered over me, his body a solid seven to eight feet tall. He was massive, his dragon tail dragging across the floor just like it had in my dream. He leaned down, his breath smelling of sulfur.

"You're a stupid little witch," he whispered. "Stupid, so so stupid. You really think I'm going to let all of them be okay? After everything they have ruined. After all the things Alex has done? All of my plans, I've had to start from the very beginning. All because you and your little coworkers have decided to ruin my plans."

I felt my stomach drop just a little, and I fought myself to keep control. To keep my cool. To keep my face from changing with horror.

"You promised," I whispered, trying my best not to sound desperate.

"A promise can be broken," Alfred said. "It's not like we signed anything. It is not like we had an agreement. Nothing that was binding. No contract, no blood oath. It's just business, Ember."

"Business?" I sneered. "Business? This is what you call business? You ruining people's lives? Monsters and witches alike, you kidnapping omegas and using their power to your own advantage. That's not business, that's just you being evil."

"Yes, I am evil," he said, shrugging. "I want power. I

want fame. I want to rule over everyone. I want to be the number one ruler, to have witches and monsters alike who will bend their knees to me. And in order to do that I have to start here. Here and now, with a little witch whose power I will use."

I started to say something back to him, but his hand shot out, his claws curling into my hair.

I let out a helpless scream as he gripped me, dragging me in my chair across the room. Pain burst through my skull, my hair feeling like it was on fire as it tugged.

I tried to squirm free, but the ropes held me tight.

He dragged me across the office and through the doorway. All the way down the hall.

Tears started to stream down my cheeks.

"Let me go!" I screamed.

It was no use. I tried to focus on my magic, but the pain was so distracting that it was hard to focus on anything else.

"You really think you're going to be able to survive this?" Alfred laughed and dragged me through another doorway into a cold dark room. He tossed me forward, the chair hitting the ground on my side, smashing against the floor. Pain radiated through my shoulder and side, his laughter echoing around me.

"You'll stay here, you'll stay here with my friend. A monster just like you, one who thought she could escape but never will," he laughed.

I still couldn't see in the dark, but I could see the doorway. And I could see Alfred pass through it, slamming the door behind him, leaving me alone in the darkness.

"Let me go!" I screamed, my voice becoming a piercing yell.

I could hear him walk away, his footsteps echoing through the hall.

I was alone.

Or was I?

"Are you okay?" A thin voice whispered.

"No," I whispered.

"I can unbind you," the voice whispered.

"How do I know you're not evil?" I asked, glaring into the darkness.

I was so fucking pissed. I wasn't done with him yet.

"Do you really think that I'm evil? I'm trapped in this room, just as you are."

Whoever she was, her voice was soothing while also sounding sick. How long had she been alone in the darkness? And who was she?

"Who are you?" I asked.

"A monster," she whispered.

I felt the ropes start to tug, the knots starting to come undone. I still couldn't see in the dark, but within a few moments, I was free.

The chair was dragged away, and I was slowly shifted to the floor. I felt several things touching me, almost like hands, ones that slowly moved me.

Pain flared through my body again, and I let out a groan.

"This was so stupid of me," I whispered. "I thought that I would be able to fight him, but things didn't go to plan."

"I thought the same," she sighed. "I made a mistake."

"How long have you been here?"

"I don't know," she said. "A week? Three days? A month? It's just darkness."

"I'm sorry," I whispered, slowly sitting up. I held my shoulder, wincing. I lifted my hands, reaching for my magic.

I could feel it, even though it was suppressed. It was right there under the surface, waiting for me.

"I can get us out," I said. "Before my mates even wake up."

"We aren't the only ones here in this building. He still has creatures working for him. And he has his assistant."

I thought about the evil assistant and scowled. "I can handle her. We're going to be okay."

We were breaking out of this fucking office, one way or another.

CHAPTER SEVENTEEN

office

LEA

I SAT UP IN BED, staring into the darkness. Minni immediately sat up next to me, the silence between the two of us speaking volumes.

"Where is she?" Minni asked.

"I don't know," I said.

I felt a hollowness in my chest, a loneliness. As if someone had cut my heart out and replaced it with something that mimicked it.

Minni rolled out of bed, already moving down the stairs with speed I simply couldn't match. I growled, reaching over and grabbing my phone off the side table.

"She's gone!" I heard Minni call.

I heard the front door slam open and tried not to think about the fact that Minni had gone out in the snow naked.

EMBER

I know you're both going to be upset, and rightfully so, but I went to the office this morning to meet Alfred. He threatened to hurt everyone if I didn't. I hope by the time you wake up, I'm already headed home. If not, then I love you both.

It felt like a punch to the gut. I felt my breath leave me, absolute dread filling my stomach.

Minni came back into my room, snow sticking to her platinum blonde hair. Her eyes were wide, her crimson irises burning with anger.

I rolled out of bed, immediately going to her. I pulled her into a hug, holding her close.

"She's gone," I whispered. "She went to the office. Apparently, Alfred somehow told her that if she didn't go, all of us would be hurt. We can go get her."

"She took your car. Why would she go without us? How did she even get out of bed without us noticing?"

"I don't know, love," I said.

I was trying to stay calm, even though Minni was only two seconds from exploding. She was worried, and I knew that she was going to take Ember leaving, to heart. For a vampire who was a tough badass, she completely fell apart when it came to those she loved.

I leaned back, gripping her shoulders. I looked down at my vampire because, yes – she was mine too.

I felt a bit of panic rise up, but I squashed it.

I had to stay calm.

"We're going to go get her," I said. "We're going to go get her, and she's going to be okay. Let's get dressed, and let's call Inferna."

"Inferna," Minni whispered. "Fuck. We have to tell Cinder too."

"Minni," I said, giving her another gentle shake. "Go get dressed."

Within a few minutes, the two of us were completely dressed. We rushed downstairs, Minni already having Inferna on the phone.

"She's gone," Minni said as we stepped out into the snow. "She left. Somehow Alfred got to her. I'm not sure how. But she said that he threatened everyone."

I could hear Inferna cursing through the speaker. I looked up at the sky, watching as the sun broke through the clouds with a strip of orange and magenta.

I was torn between wanting to spank Ember and hug her when we found her.

If we found her.

Fuck.

The thought was enough to have me stomping through the snow to Minni's car. I drowned out whatever she and Inferna were talking about as we both climbed in, my vision slowly but surely turning red.

I was hurt that she had left, but I would deal with that later. But for fuck's sake, she was smarter than this.

Still, I didn't have a looming evil monster who wanted to use me for the last few years, threatening to hurt people I cared about.

The voice of reason. My daddy had always been good at helping me find it, helping me control my temper even when I wanted to rip into others.

I turned on the car as soon as Minni shut her door and peeled out of the driveway.

"They're meeting us," Minni said quickly. "All of them. We think they're probably in that building again."

"And if she's not? Do you really think he would go back to the same building after everything that has happened? If so, then he wants us to come for her. He wants all of us to show up, and we'd be playing straight into his hands."

Minni was silent for a moment. "Lea..."

"Nope," I said, jerking the car into a sharp turn. "Don't take that tone with me. I can't handle it right now."

She let out a little breath but didn't push anymore.

"We're going to get her back," I said, gripping the steering wheel. "And then I'm going to tie her down and whip her ass until she swears to the fucking gods she will never do something so idiotic again."

"Agreed," Minni said, her voice dry.

The two of us were silent as I sped down the highway. Within a few minutes, we were in the city, and not long after— I darted into the parking garage.

Inferna, Art, and Calen were already there— looking sleepy and a little pissed off. I pulled up next to them, next to my car.

"She also took my car," I growled.

"She did," Minni said, getting out.

I took one deep breath and then got out, slamming the door hard enough behind me to bend the metal.

"Lea," Minni hissed.

"I'll buy you a new one, countess," I snarled.

"Good morning," Inferna said as we joined their circle. "Cinder, Mich, and Lora will be here soon. Alex and Anne too. Billy, Charlie, and Jaehan happened to be off today because they were going out of town until Monday."

I nodded, trying to keep control.

Inferna looked at me, arching a brow. "Oh boy. Listen, what Alfred said to her—"

"I just want to get her back," I said. "Soon. As soon as possible. ASAP, as you like to say."

Inferna pressed her lips together, giving Minni a side look.

"Don't do that," I snapped.

"I have brought coffee," a voice chimed.

I spun around and met Anne as she crossed the garage to us carrying trays of coffee.

"Thank fuck," Art muttered. "Anne, you're a blessing. Keeping monsters from murder."

"Not quite," I said, still sour.

Another car parked, and Alex stepped out, looking disheveled for once. He came over to our group, and we all formed a circle, each grabbing a cup of coffee from Anne.

"Sorry to meet like this," Minni said. "We need to find her."

"She's in the building across the street," Alex said dryly. "I'm almost certain. Alfred likes that place, and since we destroyed part of it a few weeks ago, I'm sure he's still pissed."

"Well, what are we going to do about him?" I asked. "It sounded like last time, people nearly died."

"Kill him. Banish him. Drink coffee."

"Do you want to fucking die?" I snarled.

"Okay, hold on," Inferna said, giving him a dirty look. "Useless. Our number one goal is to get Ember out and away. After that, we will plan on his demise. But we just need to get her free."

"This needs to stop," Calen sighed.

"And it will," Inferna said, putting her arm around him. She kissed the top of his head, which was unbearably cute.

Mich's car pulled in, the tires screeching as they parked.

The door was already opening, a very angry Cinder climbing out.

Minni moved next to me, the two of us unsure how this would go.

Their violet eyes were pinned on us as they came to the group, Mich, and Lora following.

"How did you not hear her leave?" Cinder asked.

"I don't know," I said. "We were asleep."

"Yeah but—"

"Cinder," Lora said, hooking her arm in theirs. "They're obviously upset too."

Cinder scowled but didn't disagree.

"Alright, we're all here," Inferna said. "Let's inhale this coffee and break into that office."

CHAPTER EIGHTEEN
search and rescue

MINNI

LEA WAS UNHINGED, and I was doing my best not to be the same.

I'd already messaged my family, letting them know I might need them if I didn't get my mate out of danger. That had led to a flood of messages, a combination of curiosity and 'just tell us when and we'll bury your enemies into the depths of hell'.

Sometimes it was nice to be a vampire.

I moved down the hall at a fast pace, the pixie demon named Lora on my heels.

We had all split up into groups. We were ready to fight, ready to do whatever was needed.

Lea, Mich, and Cinder had gone together. I was glad I was with Lora because she could keep up with how I moved.

I stepped into another room, noting the broken glass. The papers everywhere. It was a fucking dystopian mess.

Was this from when we'd come last time?

I stood still for a moment, pulling on my bond to Ember. Was she okay? She felt okay, but what if that was a trick of some kind? How did I know she wasn't dead?

The thought made me freeze, dread filling me.

"Minni," Lora whispered. "Come on. She isn't here. It's going to be okay."

I nodded silently and left the room, trying to shake the feeling of doom.

I couldn't lose her. Lea and I had just found her. We'd just been mated.

I moved down the hall, listening for heartbeats. Breathing in the scents, trying to find her.

This was a special kind of torture. Not knowing if she was okay.

Fuck.

Lora and I continued checking until, finally, I stopped.

"This floor is empty," I said, looking at her.

Lora nodded, looking around us. It was dark, aside from the bits of light that broke in through boarded windows.

Outside, it was just another early morning.

I hated that.

We should've been slowly waking up together right now. I should have been able to roll over and caress her body, to wake her up with kisses and an orgasm.

Instead, I didn't know if she was even really alive.

"If she were dead, then you'd feel it," Lora said. "Through your bond."

"What are you— a mind reader?" I asked, unable to cut the harsh tone.

"No, I just know what you're feeling right now. Come on, let's try the next floor."

With a curt nod, the two of us moved to the staircase.

We went up another floor, the echo of our footsteps the only thing I could hear.

I was searching, listening, trying to find her heartbeat.

Fuck. I was losing my mind. I was desperate. Lea was desperate too.

I wished that Lea and I were mated too.

The thought struck me as we opened the door to the next floor.

I regretted not doing so sooner. The three of us would be able to have more of a connection, and I wanted that. I wanted to spend my life with them.

All of this immortality— all of these years of being alone. But I had two mates.

I paused, a chill working up my spine.

There was something on this floor.

The scent of blood had my nostrils flaring and my muscles tensing. I looked at Lora, and she had the same look.

I looked down the hall into the darkness.

I could hear a soft click now.

Click, click, click.

I scowled. What the fuck was that?

A faint heartbeat.

I took off, barreling down the hallway at a speed only a vampire could do. I went through a doorway, following the sound, and then froze.

There were three bodies, all of them appearing lifeless but alive. I could hear their faint hearts fighting. Struggling. They were strapped down to desks, IVs hooked up to them. Their eyes were closed, and I could taste their magic.

Lora came in behind me and gasped. "Oh, fuck. Oh, gods."

They were witches.

Fuck.

Horror filled me, and we moved to them.

None of them was Ember, but we couldn't leave them here.

"He's a monster," Lora whispered. "An absolute monster. I don't understand."

I did. I felt a sour taste in my mouth, looking at the three witches.

I knew what it felt like to need to feed. I knew what it felt like to turn actual beings with souls into nothing but livestock in your mind.

Alfred didn't see any of us as equals to him. He didn't care that we had emotions, lives, or anything outside of what he wanted.

These were games to him.

"We'll get them out," I said.

"We need to call the others—"

"No," I said. "They could have found others. This could also be a trap. We're both strong. We'll get them out together."

I looked around the room again, looking up at the ceiling where a camera watched us.

Fuck.

"Minni," Lora whispered. "They're young. Like teenagers."

I felt a pang as I looked back at the witches. She was right. All three of them were barely adults. Two girls and a boy.

They were fresh. And if they were eighteen, that meant they were new omegas.

I cursed under my breath and yanked the IVs out of their arms. I tossed the boy and one girl over each of my shoulders.

I needed to get to Ember, but I couldn't leave children behind like this.

I watched as Lora picked up the other girl, waiting to see if she'd be able to carry her. The pixie demon was strong, though, her black eyes glistening with a mixture of hate and determination.

Without another word, the two of us carried them out into the hallway, heading for the staircase at the end.

The door swung open, and we both froze.

Anger and a lick of fear ran through me as none other than Alfred emerged.

"It's not very nice to steal food from someone," he said, his voice sending a chill down my spine.

Fucking hell.

I turned and gave Lora a look, one that I hoped she understood. I set the two witches on the floor and then turned to meet this bastard.

"Fuck you, you fucking ugly son of a bitch," I snarled, marching towards him. "I'm going to rip into you like a fucking sack of meat."

"Such a mouth," Alfred laughed. "I think that's an HR violation. You'll have to be punished."

"I don't work for Warts & Claws, you dick," I said.

I could hear Lora's voice working as she drew up a portal behind me.

Alfred's eyes burned in the darkness, his jowls pulling into a wicked grin.

"Sure, let them get out. You're what I want anyway."

The two of us lunged at each other, slamming into the wall. This bastard was strong but not quite as fast.

I raked my talons over his neck, trying to rip out his throat. I bared my fangs in a hiss, but he grabbed me—throwing me down the hall.

I hit the floor and rolled to my feet, watching as Lora and the witches disappeared.

Good.

They were out of danger now.

"Where the fuck is she?" I snarled. "Where is my mate?"

"Being drained just like those witches," Alfred said, stalking towards me.

His dragon's tail dragged behind him, embers burning from his mouth as he spoke.

"Those three were just to tide me over. Just enough to feed me while I waited on her. She came straight to me, thinking I'd spare those she loved. What a romantic," he chuckled.

I growled and lunged at him again. He brought his claws down, raking them over my shoulder and slamming me against another wall.

Pain burst through me, but I ignored it. I kicked at him, managing to slam my heel straight into his balls.

He let out a roar and howl, letting me go.

"I'm surprised you even have balls down there," I taunted, tackling him.

We went through a wall, the drywall and wood giving way beneath our weight.

I slammed him into the ground, only for him to grab me by the neck and jerk.

Fuck.

I felt bones break beneath his grip, and I wheezed as pain burst through me.

He started to glow, and I felt...

Magic.

Shit.

He lifted me, slamming me down on a desk. I felt blood

well, and I gasped, trying to claw out of his grip.

"You see," Alfred said. "You're just a vampire. You're not a match for something like me. In the world of monsters, there are levels of who is the strongest, and I'm at the top of the food chain. You hunt humans," he said, leaning in closer.

I wanted to vomit from his putrid breath.

"I hunt monsters. We are not the same. And this little fight was exactly what I needed to make her do what I wanted."

I glared at him as he leaned in closer, his drool dripping onto my face.

"I can't wait to watch her suffer."

CHAPTER NINETEEN

go to hell

EMBER

HER NAME WAS SYLVIA. The name of the monster who I had broken out of that room with.

It was what he wanted. He'd wanted me to break out.

Now, the two of us were hanging in chains in another room.

Sylvia was an arachnid, a woman with several spider legs that came out of her spine. She had long black hair, pale skin with a red tattoo over her chest, and she had six eyes that all blinked with misery. She also had a second set of arms.

I stared at the door, sweat rolling down my face.

The worst part about all of this was that my heat still wasn't broken. And even though I was tied up in chains, bruised and bleeding, and in a very bad place— all I could think about as the time passed was being with Lea and Minni.

"I'm sorry," Sylvia whispered. "We were close."

We hadn't been close, but I didn't tell her that.

We had made it to the stairwell when Alfred and the fucking assistant cunt from hell caught us.

"I don't know what they want from me," I said.

"Your magic," Sylvia said.

"But what about you?"

"I betrayed them, so they just want me dead. It'll be slow and painful, I'm sure."

"No," I said. "We will get you out."

The door swung open, and Alfred came in.

My breath left me as he dragged someone behind him.

"No," I whispered, bile filling my throat.

I screeched. I wasn't sure what I said, but my scream was loud enough that even Alfred covered his ears.

Minni hit the ground, coughing up blood.

Alfred slammed the door shut behind him, giving her a pitiful look.

"Your mate tried to save you," he said, shaking his head. "Pity."

"I will kill you," I whispered, my chest heaving. "I will fucking rip you apart."

"So bloodthirsty," he chuckled. "It's funny. She said the same thing. Oh, I think her words were, 'I will rip into you like a sack of meat'."

He then turned and kicked her.

"STOP!" I screamed.

Minni let out a pained groan, rolling over onto her back. I could feel her pain through our bonds, could feel it like it was my own.

My vision blurred with tears of rage.

"I told you I would hurt every single one of them," Alfred said.

"You said you wouldn't," I growled. "You said if I came here, you wouldn't. And you're a liar."

Alfred nodded, grinning. "I am. A good liar, too."

Minni let out an angry hiss, only for Alfred to kick her again. This time she rolled across the floor.

"Minni," I cried, yanking against my chains.

Alfred chuckled, letting out a happy sigh. He raised his head, breathing in the air.

"I can smell your magic, dear Ember. So passionate. So strong. You're going to give me so much power."

"I won't," I said. "I will die first."

"No," he said, walking towards me. "You'll die after."

He grinned as he stopped right in front of me, lifting his claws. Minni's blood dripped from them, and he held it to his mouth, his tongue lapping up the drops.

He held out his hand, offering me one of the claw points still drenched in blood.

"Have a taste," he said.

"No," I snarled.

He grinned more, forcing the tip of his claw between my lips. My head thrashed as I tried to turn away, but his other hand shot out and gripped my hair.

"Taste," he growled.

"*Fuck. You.*"

He was two seconds from ripping my head off when Minni popped up behind him. I screamed as her talons ripped into his eyes from behind, her crimson eyes burning with hate.

Alfred howled as he stumbled back, and the door to the room burst open.

Alex and Cinder stepped in, both of their bodies glowing with magic. Others followed them— Inferna, Art, Calen, Anne, Mich.

Lea ran through, freezing as she saw Minni hit the ground.

The others lunged for Alfred, and Lea looked up, her expression one of horror.

She ran to me, reaching up and yanking the chains out of the wall. She caught me before I hit the ground, and I yelped as she broke the other chains.

"We have to get Sylvia down," I said, looking at her.

"Go to Minni," Lea whispered, going to Sylvia.

I ran to Minni, falling to my knees next to her. She was very still, her crimson eyes almost dim.

Panic raced through me. I could feel our bond growing taut, my chest pulling with pain and fear.

I held my wrist to her mouth, hissing. "Drink. Drink, please."

Minni was unmoving.

Fuck.

Lea fell to the ground next to us, letting out a curse. She held her wrist to her own mouth, and I yelped as she bit herself hard enough to break the skin, holding her wound to Minni's mouth.

"Drink, you vampire bitch," Lea snarled. "If you don't fucking drink, I will never mate you, and the three of us will never get to be together."

I watched as Minni's eyes flashed, her lips parting. I drowned out the sounds of the fight happening around us, ignoring the way the air was burning with magic. With rage and hate and fear.

Minni drank, letting out a possessive growl. I leaned forward, pressing my forehead against Lea's.

"I can portal us out," I whispered. "I have enough magic left to draw on right now."

"Get her out."

Lea and I both looked up to see Inferna bringing Sylvia to us. Sylvia collapsed to the floor next to Minni, Inferna trying to keep the fall from being too hard.

"All three of you, and take her too. Lora is at the office with the other three she and Minni rescued. Get everyone who's hurt to Urgent Care."

I nodded, closing my eyes and pulling on my magic. I felt the familiar rush, letting the warmth swallow me. Soothe me.

We had survived.

Tears streamed down my cheeks as I made a portal.

I looked up at the rest of the room, watching as Alex, Art, Cinder, and Calen all used their magic on Alfred. Inferna, Mich, and Anne were all ready to pounce if needed.

"EMBER!" Alex thundered, looking over at me. "We need your magic!"

I looked down at Minni, but Lea gave me a little push. "Go."

I nodded, rising to my feet. My entire body ached, but I rushed to our group of witches.

Alex stretched out his hand, and so did Cinder. I took both of theirs, feeling the immediate connection.

Alex was like a vortex, drawing in all of our magic. I gasped, feeling mine almost disappear immediately. Cinder's hand tightened around mine, their voice raising.

"NOW, ALEX!"

Alex held on tighter to my hand, drawing more of my power until finally— he let go, focusing all of that energy straight onto Alfred.

He burned. My eyes widened, my knees buckling next to my sibling as we watched Alfred burn.

His howling would haunt me, but I didn't feel bad for him.

He would go back to hell, and we would finally be free.

Alfred's eyes had been ripped out by Minni, but he still looked at me.

"You will regret this," he snarled.

"Have fun in hell," I whispered.

The floor lit up with a symbol right as Alex sent all of our magic straight onto Alfred. The air was singed with sulfur and burning fur, Alfred turning into a pile of dust.

The floor stopped glowing, the howling ending.

I looked up at Alex, stunned by how much power he could wield. His eyes were bright blue, his skin almost sheer.

He let go of our magic, and I felt mine return, washing over me. I let out a breath.

Cinder immediately pulled me into their arms, holding me tight.

"Hi," I whispered, tears filling my eyes. "I love you. I'm okay."

"I was scared," they whispered. "Go to your mates and get out of here. I'll see you later."

"Okay," I said.

They pulled me to standing, and I turned, going to Minni, Lea, and Sylvia.

I was exhausted now, but I still pulled the four of us through the portal, landing us straight into the Warts & Claws office.

Everything had happened so fast, and my head was still spinning.

Alex had... Alex had banished Alfred using all of our magic.

But he had literally *taken* all of our magic.

It made me feel uneasy.

Minni groaned, finally pushing Lea's hand away. Her eyes opened, her color finally returning.

"Fucking hell," she sighed. "Ember. I swear to the gods if you ever. EVER. Leave us again, I will personally chain you in my basement. You will never see the light of day again."

My lips parted, but I was immediately pulled into her arms. I held on to her, tears filling my eyes again.

"I'm sorry," I whispered. "I'm so sorry. I shouldn't have left."

"You shouldn't have," Lea said.

I drew back from Minni, meeting Lea's gaze.

Fuck. She was really angry.

Lea stood up, looking over at Sylvia.

"Let's get her some help. Let's check on Lora and the others. And let's get ready for all of us to meet once Alex and the rest are back."

I started to reach for Lea, but she turned away.

"Lea," I whispered.

She gave me a sharp look, one that hurt worse than anything else that had happened today.

"It'll be okay, sugar," Minni said, giving my hand a squeeze. "Lea loves you, and she'll come around. Now, let's help the others, and then we'll go home and sleep."

CHAPTER TWENTY

friday, i'm in love

LEA

OUR RAG-TAG GROUP all sat around the conference table, listening to Alex speak. All of us were exhausted, traumatized, and surviving off the donuts and coffee Anne had ordered.

"Between all of our magic, we were able to send him back to hell," Alex said, letting out a breath. He was silent for a moment, his voice hitching. "Thank you. I'm sorry all of this happened."

Everyone nodded, even me.

"This has been a nightmare," Inferna said. "But, it's over now."

Alex's gaze flickered, but no one else seemed to notice. I studied him, watching his posture.

Was it over? Was it really over, and he was just processing it?

And what the hell kind of witch was this guy? I'd seen

what he had done with Ember, and it made me feel... concerned.

Minni's hand slid onto my lap, giving my thigh a gentle squeeze.

"Let's go home," she said.

I took a deep breath and nodded, standing up. "We're off. Ember, Minni, and I are going home."

Ember looked up at me, and I felt that prickle of hurt again.

I'd ignored her for the most part since we'd gotten back to the office, but once we were home...I would talk. I'd air out what I was feeling and hopefully be able to resolve the hurt between us.

"We'll see you Monday," Inferna said, smiling. "Thank you both for helping. Oh, wait. Ember."

Ember looked up at her, tilting her head.

Inferna smiled. "We haven't forgotten about your interview. When we come back to the office next week, we will set one up. Is that okay?"

Ember lit up, grinning. "Yes, please."

"Excellent. Enjoy your weekend," Inferna said.

I winked at her and looked down at Ember.

"Come on," I said.

"Wait," Cinder said, standing. "I want to talk to Ember first before the two of you take off with her."

Ember looked at her sibling and nodded. Reluctantly, I nodded too, and the four of us went out into the hall, waving at everyone else.

"We'll wait at the elevator," I said to Ember.

She nodded, and then she and Cinder walked the other way, the two of them embracing.

I watched them for a moment, sighing.

"Cinder is good," I whispered.

"They are," Minni said. "Come on."

We went to the elevator, and I leaned against the wall, exhaustion finally overtaking me. Minni stepped closer, wrapping her arms around me.

I held her close, closing my eyes.

"Thanks," I whispered.

"You hurt her feelings," Minni said.

"I'll fix it. I was just mad that she took off."

"I was too, Lea, but I didn't shove that in her face."

"I will fix it," I said. "I love you."

The words were out of my mouth before I could stop them.

Minni looked up at me, smiling. "I love you too."

"We'll all be together," I said.

"Happily ever after," Minni said, leaning up and kissing me.

I melted against her, drinking her in. Letting her touch soothe all my worries.

There was only one thing missing from this, and that was our mate.

"I'm here," Ember's voice chimed.

We both looked up, and I smiled finally. She was a little happier.

I'd missed her smile.

"Cinder would like dinner together soon," Ember said. "If everyone is willing."

I hit the elevator button and nodded. "Of course."

"I like Lora," Minni said.

"I like Mich," I chuckled, thinking about the manticore.

The bastard was as strong as an orc.

The elevator doors slid open, and the three of us stepped in. I hit the parking garage floor.

The doors slid shut, the elevator started to descend, and then it stopped.

"Oh, for fuck's sake," Minni hissed.

She reached past me, jamming the buttons.

It didn't budge.

"Damn," Ember said. "Well..."

"We'll just wait it out," I said, snorting. "This elevator is cursed."

"It is," Ember said.

I took a deep breath and looked at her, my gaze softening. "Ember, I'm sorry. I was scared this morning, scared that we wouldn't find you. Scared that you'd be dead. And when I'm scared, I get angry. That wasn't fair."

Ember's eyes immediately teared up, and she nodded. "I'm sorry too. To both of you. You could have died."

"But we didn't," Minni said. "And now that bastard is finally gone."

Was he actually gone?

"Hopefully," I said. "Regardless, we are all safe. And I love you, Ember. I love you so much, and I am thankful to have you as my mate. And Minni, I love you too. I'm glad... I'm glad that we're healing."

Ember immediately rushed forward, wrapping her arms around my waist. I held her tight, letting go of all of the dark feelings.

This day had been terrible, but we were all okay. And that's what mattered most.

I looked up at Minni as she came into our arms, nuzzling the top of her head.

"We should celebrate," she murmured.

"Celebrate how?"

She looked up at me, her crimson eyes sparkling. "Well. While I was almost dying, all I could think about was how I regretted not having a bond with you. I could feel Ember, but I couldn't feel you. And I wanted to."

I smiled, letting out a soft hum.

"Please," Ember said, looking up at both of us. "For fuck's sake, can you both bond with each other already?"

"So demanding," Minni hissed, but she smiled wider.

I grinned too. "Yes," I said. "I'd like that. And you, little lady, can watch."

"Thank you," Ember said, giggling.

With that, the elevator lurched and began to descend again.

"This fucking elevator," I said, shaking my head.

Minni and Ember both burst out laughing.

I smirked, enjoying the sounds.

Fuck, I could finally breathe again.

I took another breath, finally relaxing. Truly relaxing.

And caught Ember's heat scent.

"Fuck," I said. "Ember."

They both quieted, and she looked up, raising a brow.

"We'll fuck her out of her heat and then mate," Minni said.

"Deal."

With that, the three of us made our way home, forgetting about the work week from hell and creating a bond that not even a demon could break.

horn-y resources

ALFRED

HELL WASN'T HALF BAD. I was still able to make phone calls, even though every breath hurt, and my eyes watered as they grew back.

"Hello?" a voice asked.

"It's Aamon," I said, glaring into the darkness.

"Aamon. I heard you'd been sent back to hell."

"Yeah, that's where I'm calling from."

"They allow cell phones in hell?"

"Lucifer," I growled, glaring.

Fuck, perhaps this had been a mistake. But he owed me a favor. And when it came to such things, once called upon — they had to be filled.

He'd left this life, the one I had taken up. Alex might have sent me to hell, but I would get out.

"What do you want, Aamon?" Lucifer asked. "I have a date with my partners in about twenty minutes, and there's not a demon in hell or on earth who would keep me from it."

"I'm calling on my favor," I said. "I need out. A passage out of here."

"I don't do favors anymore," he said, his voice becoming tight.

"Are you that whipped?"

"Yes, actually, and I like it."

Fucking weak. The bastard had fallen even further than he had the first time.

"You should try it sometime. Getting laid regularly will do wonders for the soul."

"I have no soul," I sneered. "I'm calling on a favor because you owe me. I did something for you about 300 years ago. My repayment will happen now."

"Aamon," Lucifer said, his voice growing more serious. "I can bring you out, but if I do so, you'll be signing up for your death. I've heard Inferna is a formidable force, as are all of her employees. Which is how you ended up there in the first place. Why don't you cut your losses and move on?"

"NO!" I rumbled, slamming my fists down. "You don't understand," I snarled. "Get me out, Lucifer, and you will never hear from me again."

"Swear that to me, and sure. I'll get you out. But I will be telling both of my partners."

"I swear to you, Lucifer. I swear on my own soul."

"You have no soul. Swear on something else."

"I swear on his soul."

"Whose?"

"Alex. The omega witch."

"For fuck's sake. Is that what all of this is about?"

"He will either submit to me or die."

Lucifer let out a very long and dramatic sigh. "Gods.

Alright. I'll take that swear. And if you ever call again, I will personally lock you in the very dark depths of hell, in a place where cell service doesn't work. And also, if you hurt one of those connected to the family, you will also die. Understood?"

"This is about Alex," I said. "Not the others."

"Do we have a deal, Aamon?"

"Yes," I said.

"Fine. And like I said, I will be telling my partners. And I'm sure I'll get whipped for it, but that's not a bad thing."

I shook my head, glaring.

Whatever. The devil himself had fallen, but I would replace him.

I'd get out of hell and finally finish what I started.

clio's creatures

Hello Creatures!

My name is Clio Evans and I am so excited to introduce myself to you! I'm a lover of all things that go bump in the night, fancy peens, coffee, and chocolate.

IF you had the chance to be matched with a monster- what kind would you choose?!

Let me know by joining me on FB and Instagram. I'm a sucker for werewolves to this day.

P.S.

Join my Newsletter by clicking here- I won't spam you, but I will offer you fun rewards for being one of my monster loving creatures.

Clio's Creature Newsletter

also by clio evans

CREATURE CAFE SERIES

Little Slice of Hell

Little Sip of Sin

Little Lick of Lust

Little Shock of Hate

Little Piece of Sass

Little Song of Pain

Little Taste of Need

Little Risk of Fall

Little Wings of Fate

Little Souls of Fire

Little Kiss of Snow: A Creature Cafe Christmas Anthology

WARTS & CLAWS INC. SERIES

Not So Kind Regards

Not So Best Wishes

Not So Thanks in Advance

Not So Yours Truly

Not So Much Appreciated

Ingram Content Group UK Ltd.
Milton Keynes UK
UKHW011308160323
418683UK00024B/722

9 798366 382564